MARY

CLOVER SPRINGS MAIL ORDER BRIDES 2

RACHEL WESSON

LONDONGATE PUBLISHING

CHAPTER 1

BOSTON

The young girl turned to wave one last time before she stepped into the buggy. The driver clicked the reins and they were off. Tears blurring her vision, Mary continued to wave her chest aching as the buggy disappeared from view.

Moving away from the window, she slumped in the chair, tears flowing down her face. Cathy was gone. They would never again live together as a family. She clamped her mouth shut, wishing she was alone to cry properly. It had been bad enough when Katie left to become a mail order bride but that was nothing to the loss she had just suffered.

The nun turned from the window. "Control yourself, Miss Ryan. The Johnston's are comfortable and your sister will want for nothing. It is the best result for everyone."

Mary raised her swollen eyes to meet those of the Mother Superior. The color of the cold eyes gazing back at her almost matched that of her habit.

"Don't look at me that way. What did you expect me to do?"

"Nothing, Mother Superior." Mary's monotone voice hid her anger. *You could have tried harder to find a family willing to take both of us. You didn't have to send my only family to New York.*

"You look like you have something to say, child. Tell me, don't be afraid."

Mary's jaw clenched. She knew when she was being baited. She had learned the hard way that the nun standing in front of her was at her most dangerous when she appeared to care. It wasn't a trap she would fall into again. "Please, may I be excused? I have some chores to attend to." Mary sank into something between a bow and a curtsey, her eyes not meeting those of her tormentor. She gazed at the floor.

"You may go but be sure to give some thought to your plans for when you leave. Our duty to provide you with a home ends with your 18th birthday."

Mary backed out of the room. She closed the door silently behind her and slid to the floor in a heap. *Mam, why did you ever decide to come to this horrible place? We could have been happy at home. At least we would have been together.* She was so caught up in her grief, she didn't hear the nun appear.

"Mary, sweet child, do not take on so. Catherine will be happy. The Johnston's are nice people. They will look after her."

Mary looked up at the kindly face of Sister Una. She was a beautiful woman, inside and out. What on earth possessed her to become a nun? She wasn't treated much better by the Mother Superior than the orphans, yet she never once complained. She was always happy, kind and loving to the unfortunates who arrived at St. Margaret's Home for Orphans. Mary took the nun's hand and got to her feet. She brushed her skirt down and wiped her face.

"Why don't you go check on the younger children? They should be about finished now. Make sure their hands and faces are washed up for lunch."

"Can't risk a repeat of yesterday." Mary shuddered.

Sister Una shook her head, her eyes clouded with sadness, her hands clutched together as if she was praying. "What happened yesterday was awful. Sister Josephine wasn't feeling herself."

"The little ones didn't do anything. That old witch caned them for nothing and made us all watch. How can you say she was ill? She hit them so hard, she drew blood. She enjoyed it. She always does." Bile rose in Mary's stomach as she replayed the horrible scene in her mind. Corporal punishment had played its part in the Irish education system. Yesterday was the first time she had seen such savagery. Sister Joseph had accused eight-year-old twins of stealing. When they didn't admit the theft, she had caned them in front of the assembled children. Their hands were left raw and bleeding.

"Mary, control yourself. We may not agree with the actions of our elders and betters, but it is not our place to judge them."

"God said to mind the children. You know he did Sister Una. It's there in the bible for everyone to see." Mary argued but stopped. What was the point? Nobody was going to listen to an orphan. The local community didn't care what happened to the residents of St. Margaret's. Nobody did. Mother Superior was right. Cathy was lucky. She had escaped. *It will be my turn next.*

CHAPTER 2

CLOVER SPRINGS

*T*he whole Sullivan clan sat around the large dining table. Davy was hosting dinner today. They all traveled out to the ranch following Sunday Service. Davy's wonderful cook, Mrs. Higgins, excelled herself. Katie wondered if she would be willing to give her some cookery lessons. She could cook basic dishes, but seeing Daniel's reaction to the food served today made her think a couple of lessons from Mrs. Higgins wouldn't go amiss.

"So Davy, how is life treating you out here all on your lonesome?" Ma asked.

"Don't have time to be thinking about much, Ma. By the time I have all the chores done, I'm so tired I fall into bed often without taking my boots off." Everyone laughed. Katie had grown very fond of Davy.

He was always respectful to her. He treated Ellen like a little sister and the young girl adored him.

He wasn't married. Daniel had talked about a fiancé who had died some time ago. Davy hadn't been interested in anyone since, but a couple of times at previous family dinners, Katie had found him looking at her and Daniel with a peculiar expression on his face. Earlier, he asked Daniel if he and Katie could stay behind after the rest of the family went home. He wanted to talk to them about something.

Dinner went on for hours as it always did when the Sullivan clan got together. There was so much to catch up on. Elizabeth and her family lived near them in town but they barely saw each other. They were all busy with the day-to-day businesses. Ma's boarding house was nearly always full. Ma kept saying how she couldn't cope without Ellen's help.

Katie rubbed her belly. Life was so good. She was so happy, sometimes she was afraid something bad would happen. Daniel didn't take her fears seriously. As far as he was concerned, they had all the bad luck that was due to them when she nearly married Mr. Cassidy.

Finally Ma and the others left, leaving Katie and Daniel alone with Davy. Katie noticed his eyes darted around the room. He looked nervous but he couldn't be. There was only the three of them there.

"Thank you for staying behind. I really needed to speak to you and I couldn't do this in front of Ma. She would get too excited and take over everything."

Katie looked curiously at Daniel. Take over what? But her husband just stared at his brother.

"I need a wife. I can't promise to love her but I will be nice and respectful. She'll have a good life here on the ranch. Mrs. Higgins isn't going anywhere. She reckons it's about time I got myself a wife." Davy sat back, a pained expression on his face.

Katie rubbed her hands together, a huge smile on her face. "I know the perfect girl. Her name is Mary Ryan and she is one of my best friends. She came over on the ship with us from Galway. She hates Boston. This is just wonderful.

"But how do you know this friend of yours will be willing to marry?"

"She'll take one look at you, Davy, and hightail it back to Boston." Daniel laughed but shut up quickly at the glare he received from Katie.

"I can't make any promises, Davy, as these things don't always run smoothly."

Daniel opened his mouth to say something but Katie's kick on his shin was enough to silence him. "I can promise that a sweeter girl you won't ever meet. Why don't you write to Mary and ask her to come?"

"What would I say? Will you write it for me?"

"No I won't write it but I will help you. You can tell her why you want a wife."

"He needs someone to keep him warm at night."

"Daniel! You are not helping." Katie stammered, blushing intensely. Her brother-in-law would know Daniel was joking but it was still inappropriate.

"Don't mind him, Katie. He's always been the family joker."

Dear Miss Ryan

This is a difficult letter to write, given as we have never met. But Katie, my new sister-in-law has spoken a lot about you. She only has good things to say.

I live just outside Clover Springs on the ranch my Pa started when he first came to Colorado Territory. It's a busy life but a good one. I like working outdoors. To relax, I like to read. Katie said you did, too. Maybe we can compare notes on the books we have both enjoyed.

The house is too big for me alone. It was built for a family. It would be nice to hear children running around in it once more. I would love a son to pass the ranch onto.

It would also be nice to have some company, especially in the long winter months. I can't promise you love and romance. Instead I offer security. My family will never go hungry or lack shelter as long as I have my health.

I hope you are open to coming to Clover Springs and becoming my wife.

Yours sincerely, Davy Sullivan

Davy stared at the paper before handing it over to Katie. She couldn't hide her smile as she read the contents.

"What's wrong with it?" He asked, crossing his arms.

"Nothing, really." Katie's eyes twinkled with amusement.

"But?" Davy was tempted to snatch the letter back but that would be rude.

"Did you have to put in the bit about romance? You might just fall in love with her."

Davy shook his head. "There's no room in my life for love. No point in setting her up for disappointment."

He caught the glance Katie threw Daniel but he didn't want to say anything more. The less talk about romance the better, as far as he was concerned.

"When do you think she will get here? Assuming she agrees."

Katie looked at Daniel before replying. "About a month or so. I will post this as soon as we get back to town."

Davy stood watching Katie and Daniel drive off into the night. He stayed long after their wagon disappeared into the horizon. In a couple of months, he could be married. Life as he knew it would change forever.

CHAPTER 3

BOSTON

$\mathcal{M}$ary worked even harder than before hoping physical exhaustion would help her sleep at night, instead of weeping over the loss of her sister. So far it wasn't working. One evening, she was sweeping and dusting the large hall when Mother Superior came out of her office, dragging a child behind her.

"Mary, take this heathen to the scullery and give him a good wash. Burn his clothes. He is so dirty, you cannot...Ouch!"

Mary bit her lip trying not to laugh at the image unfolding in front of her. Mother Superior was almost dancing as she hopped from one foot to the other. "You little ruffian. How dare you kick a lady!"

"I didn't kick you. You fell over my foot." The boy stammered, his eyes widening at the look on the nun's face. Mary moved quickly, gathering the boy to her and rushing toward the kitchen. "I will send Sister Ursula to you Mother Superior. She can take a look at your ankle while I see to the boy." She didn't give the woman a chance to respond, opening the door to the lower floors and pushing the child through.

"You're hurting me. Get off." The boy shook Mary's hand off. "You didn't have to hold me so tight."

Mary spotted the tear filled eyes despite his tone. *He's scared, poor little mite.* "What's your name?"

The boy didn't answer, just stood there rubbing his wrist.

"I'm Mary Ryan. I'm an orphan just like you."

"I ain't no orphan. My ma and pa are still alive. They just left me here for a bit. They are coming back to collect me." He didn't look at her as he spoke but focused on a spot just over her shoulder. Her heart melted. The poor child was in denial. How could his parents still be alive and he look as neglected as he did? Sure, there were children starving in Boston but she sensed this one had been living alone for a few days at least. He smelled as if he had taken shelter in the sewer.

"Well, we best get you cleaned up before they get back. What's your Ma going to say if she sees you in this state?" Mary said cheerfully, not missing the incredulous look he gave her. She could see he wasn't sure if she believed him or not but two could play this game. "So are you going to tell me your name or will I call you Blackie?"

"Ben." The child stared at the floor. "I don't like baths."

Mary hid her smile behind her hand. "It will be over before you know it. If you are good, you can have a sugar cookie afterwards."

The child's eyes lit up as he licked his lips. "A whole cookie just for me? This is a great place to live."

Mary shrugged her shoulders. Now wasn't the time to correct him. He was better off believing that for as long as he could. Reality would hit sooner or later. As they walked toward the scullery, the boy's limp became more pronounced. "Would you like me to carry you, Ben?"

"No. I can walk." Ben stood taller but his pain was evident from the way his mouth tightened. "I ain't no cripple."

"I didn't say you were but you look tired. Now, why don't you sit for a while until I get the bath ready? I want to get you some new clothes too."

"I want to keep these ones. Ma gave them to me." He held onto his rags tightly. Mary thought quickly. "Why don't you give them to me so I can wash them? Once they have dried, you can have them back."

Ben nodded. Mary helped him undress, her heart

breaking as she noted the numerous scars across his back. Someone had beat the child and often. Fresh marks mixed with faded. Who would mistreat a child so badly? Would he fare any better here at St. Margaret's? With a deep sigh, she washed him as gently as she could. At first he shrank away from her touch but by the time the bath finished, he let her wash and cut his hair. She had to cut it quite close to his head but at least he wouldn't be shaved. With his new clothes and haircut he looked even younger. Mary couldn't resist giving him a cuddle. She put her arms around him. At first, he held himself stiffly but as she caressed his hair, he whimpered and hugged her back.

After a while she took his hand and led him to the kitchen. "You sit there. I will get you a glass of milk and that cookie I promised you. But first have some of this stew. Cook made it yesterday. It's good."

Ben shoveled the food into his mouth, causing Mary to wonder when he last ate. "Go slowly, child, or else you will be sick." She chided him gently. He slowed down but held onto his plate as if afraid someone would take it. She put the cookie on the plate in front of him before pouring herself a coffee. She took advantage of the empty kitchen to sit awhile. Her back ached from the chores she had finished before Ben arrived.

"Did your Ma leave you here?" he asked.

"No, Ben. Mam and Daddy died on the boat. We came over from Ireland but only Cathy and I made it to America."

"Where's Cathy? Does she live her too?"

Mary shook her head, fighting not to lose control. "She did before she was adopted. She left a few days ago."

He looked up at her before staring back at his plate.

"Ma and Pa aren't coming back," he whispered as he took a bite of the cookie. "They didn't want me no more. Said I would be a bur... well, it don't matter. I'll follow them."

"Where did they go?" Mary desperately wanted to hug him close but she didn't want to move for fear of upsetting him.

"Montana. Pa is going to have a farm with horses and all. Ma and my brothers have to help him build a house." Ben sniffed. "I told Pa I could work but he laughed. It wasn't a happy laugh. I don't think he believed me. It's 'cause I got a bad leg. But that don't stop me being a good worker."

Mary moved around to sit beside him as soon as his first tear hit the plate. When he didn't flinch, she took a risk by pulling him onto her knee. They cried together for a while before Cook found them.

"There you are. Mother Superior has been looking for you, Mary. Oh, who is this?"

Mary stood, putting the young boy down on the ground, but kept her arm around his shoulders. "This is Ben. He is going to stay with us for a while." She winked at cook, hoping to get the message across that the child was uncertain about living here.

"Well, Ben, aren't you a bonnie young man? Did you have a cookie yet?" Cook asked kindly.

"Yes, Ma'am. It sure tasted good."

Cook beamed while Mary smiled. It hadn't taken long for Ben to find another friend. Her smile faded. He'd need as many as he could get in St. Margaret's. "Come on, Ben, let's go see Mother Superior." At the look of fear in the child's eyes, Mary bent down to whisper to him. "Don't worry. I will be right there beside you."

Ben nodded, reaching for her hand. Together they walked slowly back upstairs. Thankfully for both of them, by the time they arrived, Father Molloy had requested a meeting with the head of St. Margaret's. Mary was told to take Ben to the dormitory for younger boys. She got him settled for the night with a cuddle and a quick story.

CHAPTER 4

*M*ary pushed the kitchen door open to find Father Molloy visiting with Cook.

"There you are, Mary. You are looking rather peaky, child. Don't you ever get out in the sunshine?"

At Mary's shrug, the Priest muttered something about having a word with Mother Superior as he fumbled with the pockets in his coat. "I have something here for you. I am not altogether sure why it wasn't addressed to you here at the orphanage."

Mary didn't look at the priest. She didn't know if Father Molloy knew Mother Superior read everyone's mail including personal letters addressed to other nuns. She wasn't about to educate him. The less involvement she had with the woman in charge, the better.

The priest sighed as he produced the letter. "Guaranteed to put a smile on your face. In fact, I am hoping I can convince Cook to pour us a coffee while we enjoy our letter."

"Our letter?" Mary couldn't help smiling at the audacity of the priest.

"Your letter, Mary Ryan, but you wouldn't spoil an old man's pleasure by denying him knowledge of the contents, now would you? I have a great fondness for Katie, who ran off to New York to visit relatives by way of Colorado Territory?"

Mary took an intake of breath. The priest knew. How?

"Don't look so worried, child. Young Katie told me herself. She wrote to me to apologize for letting me believe the story she had told her aunt and uncle." The priest fell silent for a couple of seconds. "I can't condone the deception, but that doesn't mean I don't understand her need to run. I am very happy it all worked out for her. She deserves to be happy, as do you."

"Thank you, Father. You have been so kind to us."

"It doesn't cost anything to be kind to children. God loves them – all of them, regardless of how they are situated."

Mary resisted the urge to hug the old man as she poured the priest a coffee. Pouring another for cook, she put a plate of cookies on the table and took a seat. Ripping open the envelope, she scanned the contents. She wasn't about to tell Katie's secrets, but the first few paragraphs were fit for the priest's ears. Smiling widely, she started to read.

"Dear Mary,

I so wish you were here to tell you my news in person. Daniel and I have been blessed. We are going to have a baby."

"Ach, that's grand. To be sure, she was right to marry that young Sullivan. Fine family." The priest interrupted Mary's reading as he dunked his cookie in his coffee.

"How would you know, Father? You haven't set eyes on Colorado Territory, never mind a member of the family." Cook tried her best to glare at the priest as he dropped crumbs on the table, but Mary could see she was trying not to smile.

"With a name like Sullivan, he is bound to be a first class citizen. We Irish are a proud people. A nation of saints and scholars."

Cook, being English, made a noise somewhere between a grunt and a humph. Even though the two were old friends and often allies against Mother Superior, Mary didn't think it fitting for them to continue along that line of conversation.

"Should I leave you two to have a conversation while I go read my letter in peace?" Mary made to stand.

"Don't you dare go without telling us all the news. Father here is dying to know." Cook nodded, her eyes glued to the sheets of paper in Mary's hands.

Mary went back to reading.

"Daniel is so excited but he has become a real fusspot. He won't let me out of his sight. You would think I was the first woman to have a baby. Ellen can't wait to become an Aunty. I am very proud of her, Mary. She has blossomed since we left Boston.

Enough about me. How are you? I hope you are not feeling too sad about Cathy. I know you said she was in a good home and will have everything she needs. But I can sense you are lonelier than you will admit. Now she's gone, why don't you come to Clover Springs? We would love to have you. In fact I have..."

"About time Katie suggested you join her." The priest didn't look up from his coffee as he interrupted Mary's reading.

"Of all the things to say Father Molloy. Why would a nice girl like Mary want to travel all that way out west? To be surrounded by heathens and God knows what else."

Mary laughed at the outrage on Cook's face. Before she could respond, Father Molloy got in first. "I am telling ya, there are fine people out there in that town."

"They are that, if you like murderers and bank raiders. Only by the Grace of God, Mary's young friend didn't get married to a highwayman."

Mary's coffee splashed over the table, her hand was shaking so much from laughing. A highwayman? Cook's English expressions made people laugh. "Cook, that's all behind Katie now. Her husband is a business-man. He owns the mercantile." Mary stood up to take her leave of the two old friends. "If you don't mind Father, the rest of the letter is rather private so I will say goodnight."

"You are a fine girl, Mary Ryan, to share your letters with a lonely old man like myself. Now if Cook was any sort of woman, she would be adding a drop of medicine to my coffee. She knows how this weather is bad for my chest."

"Everything is bad for your health if it's my cooking whiskey you are after." Cook muttered, getting up to find the bottle.

Mary giggled to herself, leaving the two arguing over the whiskey. She knew they would both enjoy their evening. Despite their different backgrounds, they were firm friends, united in their efforts to provide the children with as much kindness and comfort as possible. Mary walked as fast as she could to the room she shared. She couldn't give in to the temptation to run. If she was caught, the letter would be confiscated and she would be stuck.

Relieved to find the only occupants of her room were Laura and Sorcha, she threw herself on her bed and studied the letter. Her heart was beating so fast, she could barely breathe.

"Are you okay, Mary? You are breathing very fast." Sorcha looked up from her mending. She hated sewing, not least because she kept pricking her fingers. Mary usually did Sorcha's mending if only to stop everything she touched being covered in blood stains.

"Katie's written asking me to come to Clover Springs."

"Is that all? Why are you so worked up over a trip like that? I thought you would like to see your friend." Laura said, behind the pages of the book she was reading.

Mary's heart beat so fast she thought the girls might hear it. Taking a couple of deep breaths, she held out the letter. "She wants me to get married. To Daniel's brother. He wrote, too."

Laura's book dropped out of her hand onto the floor just as Sorcha gasped and sucked on her thumb.

"Marry him? Oh no, Mary Ryan. I forbid it. You can't go off to God only knows where. Not alone." Laura jumped off her bed and grabbed the letter out of Mary's hand.

"I won't be alone. Katie's there and she vouched for him. Don't you see, it's my chance to get away from here. I can be free again."

Sorcha got to her feet and did a jig. Laughing, she pulled Mary off the bed and they danced around the room. "I've been praying for something good to happen. This is it. I can feel it." Sorcha looked up at Mary. "You deserve to be happy. Once you are settled, can you find a husband for me?"

"Sorcha Matthews, you are just gone seventeen. The Nuns wouldn't let you." Laura frowned as she read Davy's letter. "Not the most romantic, is he?"

"No, but that doesn't matter. I don't need love but a place to live. A home." Mary took the letter back and read through it again. She wondered what he was like.

"So, you are going then? Just like that? Without giving it a second thought." Laura didn't attempt to hide her opinion.

Mary looked at the letter in her hand. "Yes, I am, and you're both going to help me."

Sorcha lay on her bed and sighed. "It's so romantic.

You will meet and fall in love and live happily ever after."

"Huh, trust you to think like that. It's more likely he'll be ugly, smell bad and want a slave not a wife."

"Laura Murphy. You can be a real witch when you want to." Sorcha glanced over at Mary but she ignored her. Mary wasn't bothered by what Laura said. She knew her friend was only trying to be practical, even if she had gone a little too far. Katie wouldn't let her marry someone that bad. *Would she?* She picked up some paper and a pencil.

Dear Mr. Sullivan

Thank you for your letter. It was kind of Katie to say nice things about me. She is a fantastic friend.

I have never written a letter about myself before. It's hard. Let me see. I am almost eighteen and currently living in the orphanage that has been my home since we landed in Boston.

I came over to America on the same ship as Katie. My parents wanted a new life - to be free. They both got sick and died on the journey along with my baby sister. That left Catherine and me.

Mary sucked the end of the pencil. Thinking about Cathy hurt.

Catherine has found a new family. They look after her very well but they aren't too keen on us staying in contact. They have said I can write so I guess they just don't like me visiting. I suppose it must upset Cathy as I find it hard. I don't want my little sister to forget her real family but maybe I am just being selfish.

What else do you want to know? I am not as tall or as pretty as Katie. I have blonde hair and green eyes. I guess I don't look Irish. The people in Galway used to tease my mother that she must have met a foreign sailor. I can cook, clean a house and look after little ones. I can sew but not as well as Katie.

I accept your offer to become your bride. Like you, I do not expect romance but companionship. I am looking forward to meeting you and the rest of the Sullivan family. Katie has already told me so much about them in her letters.

Yours sincerely,
Mary Ryan

Mary read back over what she had written. *Great, I sound stupid.* She passed the letter to Sorcha. Laura read it over the girl's shoulder.

"I think you do yourself a disservice, Mary. You stayed working in the orphanage to be closer to your sister. Your devotion to family and the way you are with the little ones shows you have a good heart."

Mary's eyes smarted at the unexpected praise. Laura wasn't known for her compliments. Tears slid down her cheeks causing Sorcha to rush to her side and cuddle her.

"He won't be ugly or smell bad. He will be exactly what you need. I am going to miss you, A chara mo chléibh."

Mary was surprised to feel the tears on Sorcha's cheeks. The younger girl usually kept her emotions to herself. It was her way of coping with the harsh regime in the orphanage. She hugged her back. "I will miss you too, but I will write. I will send the letters to Father Molloy. He can give them to you when he visits Cook."

"Mother Superior will be very mad if she finds out." Sorcha bit her lip as she reluctantly took up her mending.

"Who will tell her?"

CHAPTER 5

CLOVER SPRINGS

*D*avy stood by the barn, a cup of coffee in one hand and Mary's letter in the other. She'd said yes. He wasn't sure what to think now. She must be brave to agree to marry a man she hadn't met. Or desperate. Conditions in the orphanage weren't great from what Katie had told him. It was hard to get a job in Boston too, especially for a young girl with little experience. She didn't have a family to look out for her either. She was safer coming to Clover Springs. He may not be looking for love but his wife would never go hungry or be stuck for shelter.

Some female company would be good. Lord knows but he was lonesome out here on the ranch. Mrs. Higgins tried her best to fill his Ma's shoes but it wasn't a mother's love he was missing. He was a man who wanted a warm bed. He missed having a woman around to talk to. Share things with. Maybe Mary would make him laugh. He liked the way Katie made Daniel smile. His brother was a lucky man. Not that he would think about Katie in a romantic way. She was like another sister.

He looked around him. He hoped Mary knew what she was letting herself in for. Living out here on the ranch had its own trials. There were too many chores to take much time off, although trips to town had to be made from necessity. Maybe Katie could come out to visit Mary here. What was he thinking? Daniel wasn't about to let his new wife and their baby travel alone out to the ranch. Clover Springs was a nice town but the railroad had brought in a lot of new people. They didn't know everyone and the business with the Cassidy gang had shaken them all up a bit.

What was wrong with him? Standing around here fretting about someone he hadn't met yet. She had agreed to come. All he had to do was write back to her enclosing her train fare and a little extra to make sure she was comfortable on the trip.

CHAPTER 6

BOSTON

*B*linking back more tears, Mary hugged a number of the children close to her. She promised to write to them all.

"Will you tell us about Indians and snakes and ..."

Mary's tears threatened to fall in response to Ben's questions. The six-year-old boy held a special place in her heart and she hated leaving him. He wasn't likely to be adopted given his bad leg. The other children weren't always kind to him, but then, they followed the example of the adults in charge. Mother Superior plainly saw Ben as a burden and didn't bother to hide the fact she considered him useless.

Mary's heart broke for him. With love and patience, he had eventually opened up to her. Telling her stories of his upbringing and the beatings he had endured before his parents dumped him. Ruffling the boy's hair she chided him gently. "Ben, you are scaring the others."

Ben shrugged his shoulders, an obstinate look on his face. "When will I be old enough to go west? I want to be a cowboy. Can I not go with you now? You need a man to look after you. You shouldn't travel alone."

Mary hugged the little boy, her voice too choked up to speak. "One day when you are all grown up, come and visit me. You hear?"

Ben nodded, tears glistening in his own eyes. He swiped at his face. "I got chores to do." He hobbled off as fast as his limp allowed before stopping suddenly and turning back. With a look that almost broke her heart in two, he came back and hugged her with all his strength. "I love you. I don't want you to leave." And then he was gone.

As Mary walked to the train station, the image of the child's face consumed her. Leaving him behind was the hardest thing she had ever done. Since Cathy had left, Ben had become a surrogate for her family. She loved him dearly. *Maybe you could send for him? If you could convince your husband? His brother took in Ellen didn't he? But she was Katie's real sister.* One step at a time. She had to get to Colorado first.

CHAPTER 7

*K*atie came rushing out of the store as Davy pulled up outside.

"Slow down, woman, and mind that baby or Martha Sullivan will put you on bed rest." Mrs. Higgins chided Katie gently.

"I'm fine, really." Katie said breathlessly. "I have a letter for Davy." She gave the envelope to Davy who opened it slowly.

"She's on her way. She'll be here in a week."

"Your new bride. Well, praise be. The Good Lord answered my prayers." Mrs. Higgins smile lit up her whole face.

A week? Davy struggled to breathe. He felt trapped. It was too late now to change his mind and tell her not to come.

"Mary is lovely. You will fall for her as soon as she gets off that train."

"I told you Katie. It's not a love match. Don't you be getting any ideas." Davy's stomach hardened as he caught the hurt look Katie threw at him. He stalked off. What the blazes had he signed up for?

Davy was tempted to stop by the saloon. He was in for a scolding from Mrs. H on his way home. He had been rude to both women just now. He wasn't proud of his behavior but it was easier than talking about his past. *Exactly, she's the past, Mary is your future.*

Davy didn't look up as he walked off his frustration. Katie had nothing but good things to say about Mary Ryan. But nobody could be that perfect. Tilly had seemed perfect but ... he didn't want to think about her. Everyone believed he had been devastated by her death. He had loved her but the devastation she had caused was not by dying. He couldn't bring himself to tell anyone the truth. It was easier to let them believe he was overcome with grief rather than guilt and shame. He had rejected Tilly when she needed him most and it was his fault she had died. If they hadn't argued that night, she wouldn't have felt so alone. So desperate. That was something he had to learn to live with. Five years later, it didn't seem any easier than that first morning he had found out.

What would Mary Ryan expect from him? She said

she only wanted companionship but did she mean it? He hoped she did. He was done with love. Loving someone only led to heartbreak and his heart still hadn't recovered from the last time. He wasn't taking another risk.

CHAPTER 8

*M*ary looked up from the newspaper another traveler had left behind. She didn't understand all of the political commentary, but thank goodness she had arrived in the USA before President Arthur signed the Immigration Act into law. She wouldn't have been able to afford to enter America. Maybe that would have been a good thing. Her parents might still be alive and they would be together.

Mary read more of the paper in an effort to distract her thoughts of family and home. Ireland was miles away. She wondered whether the Act would have been made law if President Garfield had not been assassinated and Arthur had remained vice president. President Garfield's killer had been hanged. What would make someone kill a man simply because he was President?

Mary forced the negative thoughts from her mind as she stared out the window. Clover Springs must be close, the conductor had said they would arrive shortly. Katie had gotten her happy ever after. Maybe the same thing was in store for Mary. *Don't be setting yourself up for a fall. You aren't a bit like Katie O Callaghan. She is brave, strong willed and gorgeous. Only James thought you were pretty.* James. Why did she have to think of him now? He hadn't wanted her. Well, not for marriage. He just wanted to sow his wild oats.

A man of property didn't marry the likes of Mary Ryan. If she closed her eyes she could still hear Angela laughing. Angela, the young lady of the house had been highly amused when she realized her young maid had fallen in love with her brother. She had teased Mary something wicked when she realized the servant had been stupid enough to believe James's lies about the future they could have together. Thank God she hadn't given in to his demands to lie with him. Being poor was one thing but being disgraced was something else entirely.

Katie hadn't spoken of James. Mary didn't know whether that was because the other girl didn't know or because she didn't want to hurt her feelings. It suited

Mary, as she never wanted to think of her life in Ireland again. It was much too painful. *Why are you torturing yourself thinking of him today then? You should be looking forward to your new life.* A rancher's wife. She wondered what she would have to do? She could milk a cow. Well, sort of. The one time she had tried it; the cow hadn't kicked her so that was a good sign. She pushed the blonde hair out of her eyes, avoiding eye contact with the one other passenger in the train car. He had tried to speak to her earlier but it wasn't seemly for a young girl traveling alone to speak to a man.

Her stomach churned and despite counting backwards she couldn't relax. Would he be waiting at the station?

CHAPTER 9

*K*atie sighed looking at the clock again. The minutes were going by so slowly. She drummed her hands on the counter top willing the train to move faster.

As if to mirror her impatience, the baby started kicking. Katie smiled. Her life was completely different to what she had expected when she left Ireland. She had anticipated a life with her aunt and uncle but what she had now was so much better. She was happy, surrounded by her new family and friends. Her aunt and uncle had nobody but she didn't feel guilty. They hadn't made any effort to contact Ellen or herself never mind apologize. She wasn't going to waste time thinking about them. They were best left in the past.

Looking around the store, she almost burst with

pride. Mr. Brook would be so happy if he could see this place now. Katie had helped Daniel reorganize the mercantile. They had widened the range of stock they carried. It was sensible given the number of folk arriving by train. Some settled in Clover Springs, while others stayed for a few days before moving on with their journey.

Daniel had started keeping some items that miners would need. If they had met one person who believed they would strike gold or silver in the mountains, they had met another dozen. Katie shook her head. She was glad her man didn't have the need to go digging for gold. It was a dangerous activity.

Katie braced herself as the store door opened and in walked Mrs. Grey. The cantankerous old biddy hadn't mellowed in her attitude toward Katie. She simply ignored her as much as possible, which suited Katie fine. Daniel, on the other hand, felt slighted every time Mrs. Grey was rude to his wife.

"Morning, Mrs. Grey. Beautiful day, isn't it?"

"Rather cold, if you ask me, but then it depends on what you are used to." Mrs. Grey looked everywhere but at Katie. "Here is my list. Please tell Mr. Sullivan that he missed several items on the last one yet charged me. I do not appreciate that."

Katie gasped trying to get a hold on her temper. She would love to throw the old biddy out on her ear.

Being a store owners wife came with responsibilities. Daniel couldn't afford to lose customers, not even this spiteful old …

"Mrs. Grey, I thought I heard you. How are you today? Would you like a cookie? Katie baked them specially for … Ow." Daniel stumbled at Katie's kick.

For goodness sake, don't tell the old gossip about Mary. She has enough to contend with. Katie glared at her husband hoping he had got the message.

Daniel stuttered going slightly red as Mrs. Grey stared at him pointedly.

"I don't want any cookies, thank you. As I said to the girl…'

"What girl? Oh, you mean my wife." At Daniel's tone, it was Mrs. Grey's turn to look slightly uncomfortable.

"Yes, of course. Anyway, here is my list. I was overcharged the last time. Please do not let that happen again or I shall have to take my business elsewhere." Mrs. Grey glared at Daniel, but he continued smiling.

"If you feel you were overcharged or missing items, can you point out what these were? Katie, she's a wizard at keeping records you know, will go back over the ledger itemizing your last order and we can correct any mistakes."

Katie turned away, this time unable to hide her

satisfaction as Mrs. Grey's demeanor crumbled in front of both of them. *Take that, you old bat.*

"Do you expect me to believe you keep a record of every item you sell in this store to every customer?" Despite her tone, the old lady's hands shook slightly.

Daniel smiled, but his eyes remained cold. "Only for special customers such as yourself, Mrs. Grey." Daniel took the ledger down and made to look at it. "What items did you say you were missing?"

Mrs. Grey stammered and looked at the floor before taking a deep breath. She spoke quickly.

"Oh, it was only a few small things. Don't concern yourself, Mr. Sullivan. I am sure it won't happen again. I must rush. I have to go see about …oh, yes, the harvest festival. Here is my list. Good day to you both" Mrs. Grey almost fell in her haste to get out of the shop.

Katie waited until she was safely down the street before she burst out laughing. "Daniel Sullivan, you should be ashamed of yourself. That poor old woman…."

"Save your pity for someone who deserves it. That conniving old witch needs to learn that not everyone cares about her money. Let her take her business elsewhere. It would be no loss."

"Oh, ignore her darling. She is obviously very

unhappy. She must have had some hardship in her life to turn her that bitter."

"Katie Sullivan, what did I do to deserve you?" Before Katie could stop him, he grabbed her and kissed her soundly. Torn between letting the kiss develop and what a customer would say if they walked in on top of them, Katie eventually pulled away.

"Daniel, it's the middle of the day."

"What better time to kiss my wife and tell her I love her."

"What if someone walked in and saw us? Mrs. Grey would be scandalized."

"Maybe I should kiss her. Do you think it would put a smile on her face?"

Katie swatted him with her dust cloth. "Don't you go kissing any other woman, mister."

Daniel kissed her again. "There's only one woman for me, Mrs. Sullivan. Attractive as Mrs. Grey is…" Daniel waggled his eyebrows suggestively. They both burst out laughing.

The store door opened admitting Ma and Ellen. "You seem in high spirits." Ma said, beaming at the both of them.

"It's a beautiful day, I am married to a gorgeous woman and I have the best Ma in the world. Why wouldn't I be happy?" Daniel danced a jig.

"Have you been drinking, Daniel Sullivan?" Ma

Sullivan looked at her son, pretending to be suspicious. "Just because you are a married man doesn't mean I can't take the switch to you?"

Daniel took a hold of his mother and swung her around, causing more laughter as his mother demanded to be put down.

CHAPTER 10

atie watched as Ellen wandered over to the fabric section. Her sister's hand stroked some lovely blue material, a longing expression on her face. "It's the harvest festival soon. Will you be dancing with anyone in particular, Ellen?" Katie teased her younger sister, watching in amusement as the girl's cheeks turned crimson.

"Katie Sullivan, leave her be. Ellen will tell us the name of her beau when the time is right."

Katie chuckled as her sister's cheeks turned even redder. There was nothing like young love. "Ellen, why don't we make you a new dress? Ma told me how helpful you've been. Consider this a reward."

"Katie, really? You're the best sister a girl could have."

"How's Davy? Is he looking forward to Mary arriving?" Katie asked Ma, as she fingered different bolts of material. Daniel had escaped to the back of the store leaving the women to chat.

"I think he is, but he is trying not to be. Davy hasn't been the same since Tilly died. I hope your friend isn't expecting a lot."

"Mary is a practical girl. She knows what being a mail order bride entails, although I might have written a little of the love I found."

Ma gave Katie a hug, which she returned gratefully. She was very fond of her mother-in-law. She knew she would ensure Mary felt part of the family, too. Katie glanced at the clock. Were those hands ever going to move?

"Mrs. Shaw suggested we ask Reverend Tim to insist the festival be dry. She doesn't want a repeat of last year."

"Can't really blame her." Katie looked in her sister's direction to check she wasn't listening. " The poor woman didn't know where to look when Mr. Shaw fell over in the street. I'm not sure he'd listen. Noah would have a fit. The saloon is always full to bursting during the festivals. I think that's one argument the Reverend is going to lose." Katie looked at the clock again before drawing her sister back into the conversation. "Ellen, if you pick out the material, I will get the dress cut out before the train gets here."

"This one, Katie." The girl showed them some yellow calico.

"Don't you think the dusty pink would go better with your coloring?" Ma held the pink up to Ellen's face. "The yellow will make you paler than usual. What do you think, Katie?"

"The pink would be my choice, too, but Ellen has to wear it."

"No, the pink is fine. I need to look my absolute best."

Ma and Katie exchanged a look before they both burst out laughing.

"It's not funny." Ellen stamped her foot. "Ellie Dambridge is prettier than me. I just know he will ask her to dance." Ellen ran out the door before the adults could stop her.

Katie moved to follow, but Ma got there first. "You wait for your friend, I'll go."

CHAPTER 11

*M*ary took a handkerchief from her reticule and tried her best to remove the worst of the soot and cinders from her face. Thankfully Davy wasn't meeting her. She must look a sight. Katie had warned her about the dirt so she was wearing one of her oldest dresses. She looked out the window, excitement fighting nerves as she got her first glimpse of her new home. Clover Springs was just as Katie described it in her letters. She could see the white church in the distance. She would get married there tomorrow. She looked around curiously. There were quite a few people walking around. Was Davy one of them?

One man was sweeping the boardwalk around the entrance to what looked like a saloon. Mary shuddered. She had heard stories of other orphans ending up working in places like those. She couldn't imagine having to do that to survive. Is marrying a stranger a better concept? *He isn't really a stranger. Katie knows him and she wouldn't encourage me to marry someone who wasn't respectable.* What about love? *What about it? Didn't work out too well for you the last time did it?*

Mary started praying. *Please let it work out Father. I know you know best but I would be grateful if my husband is... .* Could she really ask for a handsome husband? Maybe one with his own teeth who didn't smell too bad. Mary smiled sadly. It was a bit late wishing he was this or that now. She would be married tomorrow. All she could do now was pray he would be kind to her.

The train shuddered to a stop and she could see Katie waiting impatiently on the platform. Excited, she grabbed her satchel bag, fixed her hat one last time and exited the train.

"I am so glad to see you. I missed you." Katie's eyes shone with unshed tears.

"I missed you too. I want to hug you but I don't want to hurt you." Mary eyed Katie's stomach.

"Come here and say hello properly." Katie pulled her close.

Mary couldn't breathe from the hug Katie gave her. She smiled. Everything was going to be fine. No matter what lay ahead, Katie would help her. She listened as her friend chattered about the rest of the family.

"You'll see Ellen later, she's minding the boarding house at the moment. Ma, that's what I call Daniel's mother, is at my house boiling water for your bath. Daniel is minding the store."

"And Davy?"

"I don't know where he is but I am sure he will turn up later. He probably got held up on the ranch."

"What's it like?"

"Big. You could walk around it but it would take forever. Davy will have to get you a horse. Can you ride?"

Mary shook her head.

"Me neither but Daniel has promised to teach me after the little one arrives. Although when I will have time for horse riding is another matter. Honestly, there aren't enough hours in the day as it is." Katie didn't pause for breath. Mary guessed it was her friend's attempt to keep her wedding nerves at bay.

"Did you get my last letter? The one where I told you I had started a dressmaking business? I didn't expect to be so busy. Turns out I don't make that many dresses but I do a lot of mending. There just aren't enough women in Clover Springs to keep up."

Mary held onto Katie's arm as they walked down the street toward the mercantile. She looked around with interest at the clapboard buildings lining both sides of the street. The majority were freshly painted, giving the whole town a clean feel. The main thoroughfare was busy with several wagons bumping along. She guessed the town wasn't usually this busy; the arrival of the train would generate extra traffic. She spotted a team of oxen dragging a wagon loaded with goods and wondered where it was going. There were a lot of people walking around too. Some children were chasing hoops down the street, running in and out behind the wagons. "It's a pretty town, isn't it?" Mary looked around her.

"It is and the people are lovely. Well, for the most part. I am not too fond of Mrs. Grey and the feeling is mutual."

"Is she the one who doesn't like you because you're Irish? Can't understand that myself. How can you hate a whole nation of people?"

Katie shrugged her shoulders. "You will see when you meet Mrs. Grey. I know Father Molloy told us that you can find good in anybody but he hasn't met her." The girls giggled. "How is Nellie getting on with Mrs. Gantley? I wish she would come here but she says she is too old to be a pioneer. You would think I expected her to go digging for gold. With her cooking skills, she'd be snapped up as a bride out here."

"Maybe that's what she is afraid of." Mary laughed.

"Nellie is in great form. She comes to see Cook quite regularly. She said Mrs. Gantley was concerned about you. She feels very guilty about what happened."

"I told her over and over that wasn't her fault. Doesn't she read my letters?"

"She did send you out here…"

"She did and I will be forever grateful. I have never been so happy. I am sure it will be the same for you, Mary."

Mary didn't believe her. Life never worked out the way she expected. If it had, she would still have her Mam, daddy and two sisters. Instead she was standing in the middle of the Wild West about to marry a man she hadn't set eyes on.

CHAPTER 12

𝒰sing her handkerchief to cover her mouth and nose from the worst of the dust stirred up by the traffic, she was glad when they arrived at the store. A handsome man was serving a lady wearing a fine calico dress. Mary fingered her own gown, wishing it wasn't quite as old and dirty. *Don't be silly. That woman hasn't travelled half way across the country on a smelly old train.* "This is our home." Katie beamed with happiness, her eyes glowing with pride. "The handsome man behind the counter is my husband, Daniel."

Daniel looked up, flashing a smile at both of them before returning his attention to his customer. Mary looked around her. Every available space was filled with goods. There were barrels of what she assumed were flour and other essentials lining one wall. The shelves above bulged with everything from bolts of material to canned goods. She guessed the heavy items for farming were stored out back, as they would take up too much valuable retail space. She spotted jars of candy on the counter and her mouth watered. What she wouldn't give now for a peppermint stick. Her breath must stink after all the traveling.

Mary followed Katie through the back of the store into the living quarters. There was a kitchen and living room downstairs. She guessed the stairs led to the bedrooms.

"Would you like to eat or have a bath first?" Katie asked before picking up the note on the kitchen table. "Ma has the water ready for your bath."

Mary's stomach rumbled, as she smelled the distinctive flavor of cinnamon. She couldn't remember the last time she had eaten a decent meal. Sandwiches didn't count. "I should say a bath but I'm starving." As if to emphasize the point, Mary's stomach grumbled again. The girls both giggled.

Mary offered to help but Katie insisted she had everything under control. She directed Mary to her room where a jug of warm water and a towel meant she could clean her face and hands before eating. She came back downstairs to find Daniel already sitting at the table.

"Please make yourself at home, Miss Ryan. We are

very pleased to have you." Daniel smiled before reaching for the biscuits Katie placed on the table.

"Thank you." Mary sat and looked at the mountain of food on her plate. She no longer felt hungry but she forced herself to start eating as soon as Katie sat down. The food smelled delicious but Mary's nerves were getting the better of her. *Why did I agree to wait? It would have been easier to get married as soon as I got off the train.*

CHAPTER 13

The next morning Katie accompanied Mary to the Church. The rest of the Sullivan family were waiting outside, an anxious expression on their faces. Mary spotted the look Daniel exchanged with Katie. What was going on? Where was the groom?

"Miss Ryan, I am afraid, well that is to say, actually…" Daniel stammered to a stop with a begging look at his wife.

Katie put her arms around Mary's shoulders. "What my tongue tied husband is trying to say is that Davy has been slightly delayed. He will be here any minute. Why don't we go back to the store and have a cup of tea while we are waiting?"

"Has he changed his mind?" *He couldn't be cruel*

enough to leave me standing in my wedding dress in the
middle of the street. Could he?

"Mary, this is totally out of character. He should be here any minute. Daniel is going to go look for him."

Mary looked around in panic but then realized how foolish she was. Any man on the street could be Davy. She didn't even have a photograph of her intended. Shoulders slumping, she turned to leave.

"Wait, he's here. He's coming. Look."

They all looked in the direction Elizabeth was pointing. Mary saw a horse racing toward them. Instinctively, she took a step backwards. The rider jumped off almost before the horse stopped. Mary's heart stopped. Or at least she thought it did. His green eyes stared at her but it was his smell that hit her first. Good Lord but he stank to high heaven! Before she could open her mouth, Martha Sullivan started shouting at her son.

"Davy. What on earth do you mean showing up at Church looking and smelling like a pigsty. It's your wedding day. What must poor Miss Ryan think of us?"

Davy didn't look at his mother; his eyes were still glued to Mary's.

"I apologize, Miss Ryan. One of my cows delivered calves and I couldn't leave her. It was twins you see and they weren't coming out properly." At the collective intake of breath Davy looked down, obviously embarrassed. "Um, what I mean to say is that the mama needed my help. If I had stayed to wash and change, you would have thought I stood you up."

Mary couldn't say anything. She was struggling not to breathe for fear the smell would cause her to bring up breakfast. She stared at him.

"Although I'm guessing you would have preferred to meet me after a bath?"

The grin he gave her warmed her heart. It reminded her of a little boy caught with his hand in the cookie jar. She nodded. He smiled back, causing goose bumps to appear all over her arms. "Oh my." She put her hand up to her mouth to prevent any more words from spilling out. Davy's mother mistook her gesture believing she was about to get sick.

"Davy Sullivan you get yourself a wash and change of clothes. Reverend Timmons will perform the marriage later if he doesn't have anything else on. Reverend?" She turned to look for the Reverend but he had already beaten a hasty retreat back into the church.

"The smell was too bad Ma, he's gone into hiding." The few guests laughed at Daniel's words but quickly dispersed when Katie and her mother-in-law glared at them.

Mary didn't notice. She was staring up at Davy, who was still apologizing.

"You look beautiful, Miss Ryan. Mary."

She couldn't reply, the sound of his voice and the look in his eyes made her want to swoon. *Swoon indeed. That's for rich ladies whose corsets are too tight. It's time I showed this town what I am made of.* "I think it's mighty fine of you to stay with your animal. She must have been frightened to death."

"She is happier now it's over. I'll show you the babies later."

Mary nodded.

"Now I best go get a bath. I hope I haven't ruined your day, Miss Ryan."

"Mary." She corrected gently. "I think you've shown me life will never be dull around you, Mr. Sullivan."

"Davy." He smiled back before nodding and turning on his heel, whistling as he walked away.

Mary stared after him until she heard Katie giggling. "Come on, little Miss star struck. Let's go and have the Irish answer to any crisis."

"A whiskey?" Daniel said, not quite hiding the hopeful look in his eyes.

"A nice cup of tea." Katie put her arm around Mary's shoulders, as if sensing she needed the support to make her feet move. *Put one foot in front of the other. Left, right, left, right.*

CHAPTER 14

*D*avy tried his best to block out his ma's voice. He'd let everyone down by arriving at the church stinking to kingdom come. But what could he do? If he hadn't stayed with the cow, the calves may have died. He couldn't afford to take that chance. Not even for a stunning blonde. Had Katie mentioned how gorgeous her friend was? He couldn't remember. She wasn't classically beautiful. Her nose was a little too big and her chin stuck out slightly but her hazy sea green eyes sucked him in from the moment he set eyes on her. The men in Boston must be blind. He scrubbed his neck and behind his ears. Without a by your leave, his Ma entered the room and dumped a bucket of cold water over his head.

"Ma!"

"Hope that knocks some sense into you. I have

never been so embarrassed in all my life. Thank God your father isn't here to witness this."

Davy opened one eye to see his mother standing beside the bathtub with her hands on her hips. It had been a long time since he had seen her so riled up. He started to laugh.

"What's so funny might I ask?"

Davy couldn't answer. He tried not to laugh. Snorting, he tried to escape under the water.

"Did that cow kick your head when you were delivering those calves? You seem to have lost your mind."

"Ma, get out of here and let me get dressed."

'I'm going but you listen to me, David Sullivan. You get yourself dressed and over to that Church. I wouldn't blame the poor girl if she took the next train out of here."

CHAPTER 15

*M*ary sat half listening to Katie and the others as they chatted. She knew they were trying to take her mind off the fiasco this morning but it was all she could think of. Well, not all. He was so handsome. She never dreamed a man like that would even look in her direction. *Well, he didn't, did he? He sent for you because he needs a wife.* Her skin tingled as she thought of how tall he was, how muscular his arms looked. He was every inch a cowboy.

She had seen the way he looked at her. Her hands shook. For the first time, it dawned on her she would have to go home alone with him. Would he expect her to share his bed tonight? Maybe he would be kind enough to give them some time to get to know each other. She knew very little about what happened between husband and wife. Mam had always said it was time enough to learn before she got married. Now time had run out and Mam wasn't around to explain. No point in heading down that road, she would be in floods of tears before too long. She had to concentrate on the present. Maybe Katie would tell her. Mary had seen the private looks Katie and Daniel had exchanged when they thought nobody else was looking. They were obviously very happy together. Would she and Davy be like that? A knock at the door startled them all. Katie stood to answer while Mary wiped her hands down the sides of her dress. She recognized his voice. Is he here to cancel the wedding? Her heart fluttered but thankfully she didn't have time to wonder if it was worry the wedding would be cancelled or anticipation of a future beside Davy.

"Miss Ryan, I apologize for this morning. I hope you still intend to go through with the ceremony."

Mary stood. "I agreed to be your wife."

"Well, yes, of course. Shall we go?"

Mary panicked. She wished she had the guts to ask him to wait for a couple of weeks to marry until she got to know him better. But where would she stay? The boarding house was full. Katie would offer her a room but that wouldn't be fair. She had enough on her plate with the store, the coming baby, and not to mention the fact that she hadn't been married long herself. No, there was nothing for it. She had to get married today.

She stood up just as Daniel came over to her. "I would be honored to give you away. I know we just met but Katie has told me so much about you. I feel like I already know you."

"Thank you." Mary couldn't say anything else. Her mouth had gone so dry she wondered if she would be able to answer the priest. The priest. Where was he? She hadn't seen him this morning.

CHAPTER 16

*W*alking slowly, Daniel pointed out places of interest in the town but Mary wasn't listening. Her stomach was going round and round and she struggled to not give in to her instinct to flee. As the church loomed over them, she stopped.

"Are you all right, Miss Ryan?"

Mary didn't respond immediately. She needed a minute to compose herself. She had dreamed of her wedding but it was nothing like her dream. Her Mam and Daddy weren't there. She was in a strange town about to marry a man she had only exchanged a few words with.

"Miss Ryan, please don't look so worried. My brother is one of the kindest men I know. He messed up this morning, but surely the fact he wouldn't leave an animal to suffer alone gives some indication as to the type of man he is?" Mary couldn't say anything. She opened her mouth but nothing happened. "He will be nice to you and, in time, I hope you are as happy as I am with Katie."

"Thank you, Daniel. Katie is a lucky woman." Mary finally found her voice.

"I think I am the lucky one, Miss Ryan. Now shall we go inside?"

They walked slowly up the steps and into the church. Where was the holy water? The smell of incense? The priest?

DAVY TURNED to look at the vision gliding up the aisle. She seemed to be floating not walking. Her eyes were glued to the floor, her pale face a stark contrast to her dark green gown. *She's petrified.* Davy took a step toward her, causing her to look up. Her eyes, full of fear and trepidation, made him want to reassure her. It would all be fine. He wasn't going to make a nuisance of himself. They might be getting wed today but, for the time being, it would be in name only. He wasn't going to jump on the poor girl the second he got her home. Was that what she was thinking? *How would you*

know? She's a stranger. He took her hand and rubbed it gently, trying to show her he understood her fear. She glanced up at him and gave him a half smile. She had spunk.

THE WEDDING CEREMONY passed in blur. One minute she was walking down the aisle as Mary Ryan, and the next thing, her husband was told to kiss her. Mary looked up shyly at her groom. She didn't have long to wonder about the kiss as his lips met hers. It wasn't a long kiss, thank goodness, as the effect made her want to swoon again. She liked the feel of his lips on hers and missed them when he moved away. He took her arm and they turned to face their friends and family. She couldn't help smiling.

The wedding breakfast, although it was now nearer teatime, was held in a café just down the street from the church. Davy didn't leave her side. She was surprised at the number of people who had turned up from the wedding. It seemed her husband and his family were well respected in the town. *Her husband. Mrs. Mary Sullivan.* It sounded right.

As if he could read her mind, Davy looked into her eyes. "How are you feeling, Mrs. Sullivan?"

"Fine, thank you, Mr. Sullivan."

He laughed. She liked the sound of his laughter and the fact he had a sense of humor. Mam always said to avoid moody or mean men. He didn't seem to be either given his laughter and the number of guests at the meal. She hoped people would forgive her for not remembering their names. After her long journey and sleepless night last night, she was tired.

"Are you ready to go home, Mary?"

"Yes, please." She said, smiling shyly.

To some good-natured teasing, they said their goodbyes. The guests escorted them to Davy's wagon. Katie hugged her and kissed her on the cheek. "Everything will work out. I promise." She whispered into Mary's ear before stepping back to link arms with Daniel.

"I hope you will call me Ma as well. Katie does and I love it. You are very welcome to our family, Mary. Mrs. Higgins will look after you. She is a wonderful cook. I have put a basket of foodstuffs and other necessaries in the back of the wagon to tide you over until you get settled." Martha gave Mary a warm hug.

"Thank you very much, Mrs. Sullivan, I mean, Ma." Mary returned the older woman's hug. She was about to climb into the wagon when Davy came over to assist her. "Wrap this around your legs, we don't want you getting cold on the way home."

It was really nice to have someone so considerate for her comfort. Mary took the blanket eagerly. She was shivering but whether that was from being cold or scared, she wasn't going to think about.

CHAPTER 17

*A*fter saying their goodbyes, the wagon rolled off toward home. She clasped her hands on her lap trying to calm her nerves. She wished Davy would say something but he seemed to be thinking. Looking up, she saw the stars shining brightly. *Mam, if you are up there, please help me.*

"Lovely night, isn't it?"

"The stars are so bright out here. Do you live far from town?"

"About an hour or so. Do you know how to ride?"

"A horse?"

"Well, unless they ride cattle in Ireland." Davy laughed, but at her silence, he stopped. "Yes, a horse."

Mary cursed her stupidity. "I'm a fast learner."

They continued in silence for a bit. *Say something?*

Anything? When it became apparent she would have to make conversation, she said, "Your Mam is very thoughtful. Who is Mrs. Higgins?"

"Mrs. Higgins is my cook. She is the best house-keeper in the whole of Colorado territory. Wait till you taste her cooking."

"You have a housekeeper?"

Davy nodded.

"Oh."

"What?"

"I thought, well, I mean I assumed…"

"Go on, girl, spit it out." Davy smiled at her before turning his attention back to the road ahead.

"Most men who order brides want housekeepers or cooks."

"I already have a housekeeper who is a great cook."

So why do you want a bride? Mary was dying to ask but maybe she didn't want to know the answer.

DAVY SHIFTED IN THE SEAT, uncomfortable at the turn of the conversation. He thought Katie would have told her about Mrs. Higgins. If he had wanted a cook, he could employ one. He wanted a wife for companion-ship. Someone to keep him warm at night. He wanted a family. It seemed obvious to him but he didn't want to spell it out now. His new bride was as skittish as a colt.

"Mrs. Higgins would have come to town for the wedding but she's been feeling a little under the weather. I told her to rest. In fact, I ordered her to bed. Told her I would fire her if she set foot in town."

"Oh, the poor woman. You probably frightened her to death."

Davy burst out laughing. "Not likely. You haven't met Mrs. Higgins. If anything, she is the one who frightens me." He sensed Mary didn't believe him but she would find out for herself. The thought of Mrs. Higgins being frightened of anyone, least of all himself, made him smile. The woman was the bravest person he knew. Hadn't she defended her homestead against a band of murdering Indians almost single handedly? She hadn't fallen to pieces when her husband was shot dead at her side. Thankfully the army had arrived in time before she had run out of ammunition. But not before she had avenged Mr. Higgins. Davy had met her shortly afterwards. She had come to Clover Springs with her twin boys and Ma had employed her straight away. The boys, Aaron and

Samuel, had grown up with the Sullivan clan and were almost like brothers.

He glanced at Mary, who sat stiffly by his side. Now wasn't the time to tell her how Mrs. Higgins came to Clover Springs. In his experience, most folk from the East were terrified of Indians.

CHAPTER 18

*H*e spotted the ranch in the distance. He sighed contentedly. He was a lucky man. He had a nice house but the woman beside him was going to turn it into a home. He found himself picturing the kids they might have. *Dark haired boys and blonde haired girls. How many would they have?*

"Are we nearly there? I thought I saw lights up ahead."

"Yes, Mary. Almost home. How are you feeling?"

"Fine."

"Really? If I were in your shoes, I would feel a little scared." He silently cursed the minute the words were out of his mouth as her whole body stiffened at the implication.

"Do I have reason to be apprehensive?" She blinked rapidly.

"No. What I meant was… Well, I can't imagine going to live somewhere I had never seen. I was trying to be understanding but I messed up. I'm sorry."

Mary made a suspicious sound.

"Are you laughing or crying?"

"Laughing. Sorry."

"I was only trying to be nice."

He could see she made an effort to stop laughing. It didn't entirely work.

"Maybe you are trying too hard."

"Maybe I am." Davy scratched his chin. "I guess I am nervous, too."

He pulled on the reins as the door to the ranch opened. Never was Davy more delighted to see someone.

"You should be in bed." He said as he greeted the older woman.

"That's a fine greeting, isn't it? Where are your manners? You could at least lift down your new bride and introduce her to the staff."

"Yes, Ma'am." Davy jumped down and walked over to the other side of the wagon to help Mary. He put his arms around her waist and swung her down to the ground. Her sweet perfume smelled good. He drew her closer and kissed her gently on the forehead.

"Mrs. Sullivan, welcome to your new home."

Davy smothered a laugh as Mrs. H pushed him aside in her eagerness to meet his bride.

"Oh aren't you the bonny one? Good thing you are married already or my boys would be all over you. Come inside, child, or you will catch you death. Davy, grab the bags."

"Now do you see why I am more scared of her? She orders me around as if I was one of her sons."

"You coming or going to stand there all night bellyaching?"

Mrs. Higgins took Mary by the arm. "Come on. I have dinner ready. You are bound to be hungry after your long day. I am sorry I missed your wedding. Someone had to hold the fort out here. With the boys away, it was only Henry and me. He doesn't do much so there you have it."

Davy snorted. Henry, his right hand man, wouldn't be too happy to hear Mrs. Higgins dismiss him so casually.

CHAPTER 19

Mary looked around her new home. It was lovely, bigger than she had imagined. Mrs. Higgins gave her a tour of the house, chatting away the whole time. There was a huge open fireplace in the sitting room, a table with eight chairs in the dining room and a large kitchen. Upstairs, she had counted four bedrooms.

"Is one of these your room, Mrs. Higgins?"

"Oh no dear, I don't live in the house. I have my own little home just out the back there. You cannot see it now as its dark."

"You mean all this is just for Davy?"

"Yes, well, it was the family home. Old Mr. Sullivan, bless his soul, came here years ago. He built a smaller house but it was pulled down and this larger one built when the Master and Mrs. Sullivan were wed. I didn't live here then. When I arrived, Davy was about five. Daniel was two or three and Martha was pregnant."

Mary listened or at least she tried to. If Mrs. Higgins went home to her own house that meant she and Davy would be alone. Her heart beat faster as Davy walked back toward them.

"I put your bags in the bedroom. I will have to leave you with Mrs. Higgins until I see to the animals. Are you all right?"

She looked at her husband, seeing concern in his eyes. Did he think she wasn't up to all this? "I am fine, thank you."

"Henry has seen to the animals. Why don't you sit down with your new bride and eat your dinner." Mrs. Higgins brushed her hand across the table as if to remove some dust.

"Don't fuss. I will be back in ten minutes. I want to check the calves." Davy ran before Mrs. Higgins could argue.

"Like a new father he is, the way he fusses around those calves." Mrs. Higgins tutted, not seeming to notice the fire in Mary's cheeks at the thought of Davy being a father.

"Why don't you sit down, Mrs. Sullivan?"

"Mrs. Higgins, please call me Mary. I look for Davy's ma when I hear anyone say Mrs. Sullivan."

"I can't be calling you Mary but I will settle for Miss Mary. Would that work for you?"

Mary couldn't believe she had gone from being a servant in a big house to being the mistress of this ranch. She touched the gleaming wooden dining table.

Davy returned as promised, water still glistening on his face. He had obviously washed up for dinner. He smiled as he took his seat opposite her. Although the dining room was huge, the candles Mrs. Higgins had set on the table made it appear quite intimate. She served both of them. Mary's mouth watered at the delicious smells. She had been too nervous to eat after the wedding.

"Now, I have left dessert in the warmer and coffee on the stove. Have a good night and I will see you first thing in the morning."

"Good night Mrs. H but I insist you stay in bed until at least noon. We intend sleeping in, don't we, Mary?" Davy said cheerfully as he picked up his fork.

"Do we?" Mary couldn't keep the panic out of her voice. Desperation made her daring. "Mrs. Higgins, why don't you stay a while and chat with us?"

"Not tonight, dear. Newlyweds need some time alone."

With that she was gone. Mary turned back to her husband. He was eating as if it was his last meal. She picked up her fork but her appetite had vanished. Her hand shook slightly so she put the cutlery back on the table.

"I thought you would be hungry. You should eat something. Keep your strength up."

Bile rose from Mary's stomach. What did she need to keep her strength up for? Oh dear God, what had she done. She stood up quickly, causing him to scramble up as well. "Sorry, please sit and eat. I am very tired. Would you mind if I went to bed?"

"This early? I thought we might sit a while. Mrs. H lit the fire in the sitting room. It should be quite cozy now."

Mary stood staring at him. She couldn't conquer the fear in her stomach.

DAVY LOOKED AT HIS BRIDE. She looked like a deer caught in a trap. The poor girl was terrified. He was such a clutz. "Mary, please sit down and eat something. You will feel better." To his relief, she sat but didn't reach for a fork. He picked it up for her and spearing a morsel of steak on the fork, lifted it to her lips. "Try this. It's good." He said softly. She opened her mouth taking the meat delicately. He had to look away. She was so kissable. He continued to feed her for a little bit in silence.

"Mary, um, well I…" Davy stammered.

"Yes?"

Darn it but the wariness was back in her eyes. He had to get her to trust him otherwise it was going to be very uncomfortable for both of them.

"I just wanted to make sure of the sleeping arrangements." Davy fiddled with his collar. This was harder than anything else he had ever done. She wasn't making it any easier. Her cheeks were rosy now, flushed with embarrassment he guessed. It made her look even more attractive. "I thought you might prefer to take the larger room. I will sleep in my old room for now."

"You will?" She stuttered but he didn't miss the hope in her eyes. He nodded, causing her to close her eyes and take a deep breath. "Thank you."

"This is all new to both of us. I think we should wait until we know each other a little better before we have a real marriage."

"A real one?"

"You know." At her look of confusion, he took a deep breath. Would he have to spell it out for her? "I know we are married but there is no rush is there?"

Mary shook her head. Relieved that was over and

there was no further misunderstanding, Davy stood up and started to clear the table. "Do you want to have coffee in the sitting room or would you prefer to go to bed?"

"I will help you clear first, then coffee would be nice."

Together they cleared the table, washed and dried the dishes.

"Mrs. H will be pleased. She is always complaining I don't wash up after myself."

"I guess you are busy on the ranch although you might have to tell me what you do?"

"Why don't we go in by the fire and sit a while?"

Talking to her was so easy, Davy didn't realize how much time had passed until Mary tried, but failed, to stifle a yawn. He stopped.

"Sorry. I didn't sleep very well last night."

"It's me. Once I get talking, I never know when to shut up." Davy stood and held out his hand to her. He walked her toward the stairs. He felt her stiffen; her nerves were probably getting the better of her as he walked her up the stairs. *She is so brave. Coming all this way to wed a stranger and finding herself all alone with him at night. She must be terrified.* Tenderly, he squeezed her hand hoping his touch would help settle her. They came to a standstill outside the bedroom door.

"Goodnight, Mrs. Sullivan."

"Goodnight."

It was no use; he had to kiss her just once. He had been patient all evening and it was his wedding night after all.

CHAPTER 20

*R*elief swamped her. He'd said goodnight and didn't appear to want to follow her inside. She turned to go into the room but his hand stopped her. Turning her gently toward him, he brushed his lips against hers. Her heartbeat quickened as she moved closer to him. She tilted her face not wanting the kiss to end. With a moan, he gathered her closer, the pressure of his lips making her open her mouth. She jerked in surprise as he deepened the kiss. She savored the sensations. Surprised she found she liked it. A lot! He pulled away.

"Please go to bed now, Mary."

She nodded, her tongue licking her lips, her eyes glued to his. *Kiss me again please. She couldn't kiss him. That would be too forward.* He looked at her for so long, she thought he was going to grant her wish but instead he grazed his lips across her forehead. "I have to go." He stalked off, leaving her wondering what she had done to upset him. Maybe he doesn't like kissing me?

DAVY ALMOST RAN DOWNSTAIRS and out the front door. Telling himself he needed to check the calves once more before turning in for the night. The kiss had shaken him. He didn't intend for it to go that far. It should have been a goodnight peck on the lips. Thank God they were already married. He had promised himself he would give her time to get used to being around him before they shared a bed. But after that kiss, he wasn't sure he would be able to keep his promise. She was totally innocent of what took place between a man and woman, of that he was sure. But her reaction to his kiss had suggested his new wife had a passionate nature. He couldn't wait until this became a real marriage.

But didn't women want romancing? He wasn't in love with her. That wasn't part of the deal. Love only led to heartache. He had experienced that once and didn't intend ever to go down that road again. Too hot and bothered now to think about sleeping, he decided to do some chores. There was always something that needed doing around the ranch. Hard physical labor would be just the ticket to take his mind off the lady he had just left.

MARY LAY in the bed going over and over the kiss. She closed her eyes, reliving every moment as she cuddled his pillow. His scent. Maybe this marriage would be like Katie and Daniel's after all. She had been kissed before. James had often taken advantage of the fact that as a servant she was often left alone. Many a kiss they had shared but it had never resulted in the feelings she had tonight. When James had tried to deepen his kisses, her stomach had roiled in protest. Yet Davy's kisses left her wanting more. She had almost begged him to kiss her again. Shame overcame her. What would her parents think if they knew she had behaved so wantonly? But then they had been young and in love once, too. In love? She wasn't in love. They had only just met for goodness sake. Tossing and turning she tried her best to fall asleep.

"Good morning, Miss Mary. Beautiful day it is, too."

Mary groaned as the housekeeper opened the drapes flooding the room with sunlight. She shot up in the bed. Just how late was it? The sun looked like it was high in the sky.

"Don't look so scared, child. It is normal to sleep late the morning after your wedding night. I hope Mr. Davy didn't keep you up too late."

Mary's cheeks flushed at the implication but she didn't get a chance to respond. Mrs. Higgins was fussing around the room, straightening the covers. "Would you like breakfast in bed?"

"No, thank you, Mrs. Higgins. I will get dressed and be right down."

"Why don't you call me Mrs. H like Davy does? Mrs. Higgins is a mouthful, isn't it?"

Mary smiled as the housekeeper left the room. She stretched before getting dressed into one of her two day dresses. Neither was really suitable for her new role but they were all she had. Her wedding dress would be kept for Church. She walked slowly down the stairs, wondering where Davy was. Then she heard him joking with the housekeeper.

"Good morning, beautiful." He stood as she entered the kitchen moving toward her to lay a kiss on her cheek.

"Morning." She stammered, his nearness causing her pulse to beat faster.

"You looked so peaceful, I thought it best to leave you sleep late." His wink told her his comments were for the housekeeper's benefit.

Embarrassed, she looked at the floor.

"I thought we might go into town and buy you a few items. Some new clothes, for instance."

Shame overwhelmed Mary. He had obviously taken one look at her dress and seen how poor his new wife was. Davy didn't appear to notice her embarrassment.

"You need a riding dress for one thing. We don't have sidesaddles so you may as well learn to ride astride. Katie may have some split riding skirts in the store. If not, she can make one for you. Unless you can sew too?"

"I can but not as well as Katie. She could sell the dresses she makes."

"I think that might have been the plan but maybe after the baby. Ma can't wait to get her hands on another grandbaby."

Mary blushed. Was he hinting he wanted to start making a family? He said he was willing to wait. Had he had a change of heart? Did she mind? She was so caught up in her own thinking, she completely missed what he said next. He was staring at her. *Lord, he will think I am soft in the head.*

"Sorry. I was miles away. What did you say?"

"I asked if you would like to go visiting with Katie while I check on some other business in town."

"Thank you. I would like that."

"Great, I'll go get the wagon. Mrs. H can give you a list of whatever she needs us to get at the store."

Mary was thankful Davy had bundled up a blanket for her to sit on. Her rear end was still sore from the trip yesterday. She guessed she would get used to it. She glanced at Davy willing him to break the silence but he was staring ahead at the road.

"What's it like working on a ranch?"

"It's hard work but I love it. I like working for myself. I couldn't work in town all day long, especially somewhere like the store."

Mary looked around her at the wide open spaces leading up to the distant mountains. "It looks really peaceful out here."

"It is mainly but you wouldn't want to go out on your own. I will accompany you where possible. Can you shoot?"

Mary stared at Davy, her mouth hanging open.

"Don't look so frightened. You will be safe at the ranch but just to be sure, I want you to be able to protect yourself. So can you?"

"No. I couldn't shoot anyone."

"Might not be a person. You could be faced with a grizzly or a rattler."

Mary's knees would have buckled if she hadn't been sitting on the wagon. She looked around her wildly. A bear wouldn't come so near to the ranch, would it?

"Don't look so scared. We haven't had a grizzly nearby for years."

"Why did you have to mention it then?" She threw him a dirty look but it only made him laugh.

"You aren't in Boston now. Out here everyone needs to know how to handle a gun. Never know when it might come in useful. We will pack a picnic and have some fun."

Mary was saved from answering as they arrived in town. Davy pulled up outside the mercantile. Before she got a chance to step down, he was standing in front of her. "Allow me." Reaching upwards, he put his hands around her waist and lifted her effortlessly to the ground.

Mary shivered at his touch. She didn't want him to let her go. He seemed to agree as they stood for a few seconds outside the store. He was looking down at her. She found herself gazing at his mouth, remembering the kiss they had shared last night. His eyes darkened as she moistened her lips. The moment was broken when Daniel opened the store door.

"Are you two lovebirds going to stand there all day or are you coming in?"

Davy released Mary with a sigh. "Go on in. I'll find you after I complete my business."

"Katie put the kettle on when you pulled up outside. She's upstairs. Go on up." Daniel said as he moved to serve a customer waiting at the counter.

"What took you so long? You pulled up ages ago. If I had known it would take you this long to come in, I could have made cookies to go with the tea."

Mary's cheeks flushed even more at Katie's teasing.

"Well Mrs. Sullivan, it's easy to see that marriage suits you."

"Katie, stop it. You're embarrassing me." Mary took off her shawl and sat at the table.

"Where's your husband?"

"He said he'll pick me up later. He wants me to get some clothes. He took one look at my dress and announced we were coming to town." Mary looked down at the dress. It was rather shabby.

Katie poured the tea. "He's like Daniel. Generous to a fault. We have a couple of dresses in your size in the store. You have your tea and I will get them. We'll need to see if they need altering."

Mary enjoyed Katie's company. Ellen stopped in at the store after school.

"I am making Ellen a dress for the Harvest festival. You'll need something to wear too, Mary. Everyone gets dressed up. It's a celebration for the whole town."

"There is food and competitions and dancing. Last year's was wonderful This year will be even better."

Ellen's face lit up. "Katie, can I please try on the dress again?"

"I haven't sewn anymore since yesterday."

Mary smiled at the sisterly teasing, wishing Cathy was in Clover Springs. She didn't want to upset the others so she didn't say anything. Katie squeezed her hand anyway. Her friend didn't miss much. All too soon Davy arrived back to escort Mary to the ranch. Katie parceled up the clothes they had picked out while Davy settled the bill.

"See you at Church on Sunday."

"Bye and thank you."

CHAPTER 21

ary curled up on the chair nearest the fire. She had a book in her lap but had given up trying to read it. Her thoughts were too jumbled up. His voice startled her making her stomach turn over.

"You like to read?" Davy asked, warming his fingers in front of the fire.

"Oh, yes, but I didn't get much of a chance to at the orphanage. Back in Ireland, I worked at the big house. The master had a library and allowed us servants to borrow books. He believed all people should be educated. He was different from most of his class."

"Why? Because he lent you books?"

"You have no idea what it was like in Ireland. The majority of the wealthy landlords were opposed to teaching their staff anything, let alone allow them to borrow books. They wanted to keep people ignorant and poor so they wouldn't rise up against them. Kind of backfired on them though. There is only so much cruelty and unfairness people will put up with. Then they start to rebel." Mary shuffled in her seat. Maybe Davy wouldn't approve of being married into a rebel family. She should have stuck to the version of truth she told Katie. The other girl had believed Mary's family had gone to America under the assisted package system offered by some Irish landlords. Mam had told everyone that story so they wouldn't take against the family. She didn't want her husband to be refused admission to America. Daddy had died, followed by Mam and the baby, but still Mary hadn't told Katie her parents had lied.

"Were you part of the rebellion?"

Davy's question brought Mary back from her memories. "My father was a member of the Irish Republican Brotherhood and therefore, we were all guilty. Daddy had to leave Ireland in a hurry. Otherwise he could have been arrested, or shot. Mam wanted the family to stay together so we all came over to America. Well, only Cathy and myself arrived. Daddy got fever and Mam died after having my little sister. They were all buried at sea."

Mary stared into the fire but she wasn't looking at the flames. She could see the wrapped bodies being lowered over the side.

"And Cathy? Katie said something about your sister being adopted."

"Yes, she was adopted a few months ago. Her new family are well off. They spotted Cathy at church. She looks like an angel and sings like one, too." Mary sniffed, causing Davy to stroke her back. She liked the feel of his hands but it made concentrating on his questions difficult.

"Could they not have offered you a home too?"

Thank goodness they didn't. Then I wouldn't be here with you. Mary's face flushed. She wasn't sure if she had verbalized her thoughts. But Davy was waiting for an answer. She took a deep breath.

"No, there wasn't any room in their lives for an older girl. Cathy was only 12. She was very unwell on the voyage over. Her new family can provide her with everything she needs."

"But not her real family. That must be difficult for you."

"It was but it gets easier with time, I think. Katie was very kind to me. She is like another sister. And Ellen too, of course." The conversation was getting too intimate and she didn't want to start crying in front of her new husband. She didn't want to go to bed though either as she was enjoying his company. Frantically she looked around, the books prompting her next question. "What books do you like reading in particular? You have so many in the house."

"I love Charles Dickens. A Christmas Carol is one of my favorites but don't tell anyone. I have a reputation to consider." He waggled his eyebrows as he joked.

"Oh, with Tiny Tim. I loved that story, too."

"I guess you thought I would prefer more manly stories. Like 'A Tale of Two Cities' for instance?"

"I enjoyed that, too. It was very romantic." Mary sighed, tiredness and relaxation made her lean backwards, right into his chest. His arm fell around her shoulder as he moved closer.

"Romantic?" He breathed, his eyes glued to hers.

Mary's heart beat faster, she was having difficulty breathing never mind speaking. He was so close. She looked at his lips, wondering what it would be like if he kissed her again. "Well, umm, yes, the hero…well, saving those people and trying to comfort the young girl." Mary gave up trying to think. She closed her eyes, waiting.

The only sounds in the room were the crackling of the fire and their breathing. The rest of the house was silent. Mary shivered but it wasn't from fear.

"Is that what you are looking for, Mary? A hero?" He whispered so close to her ear, she was sure his lips kissed her hair. Well, as sure as she could be. It could also be wishful thinking on her part. He was flirting with her. She hadn't imagined that.

"Maybe. Isn't every girl?"

CHAPTER 22

*M*ary rose early to find Mrs. Higgins already in the kitchen. The delicious smell of bacon frying filled the room. Mary watched Mrs. Higgins work. She had two skillets on the stove, one for the eggs and the second for the bacon.

"Mr. Davy he likes his bacon crispy. He also prefers the potatoes cooked in the bacon fat." Mrs. Higgins chatted as she deftly sliced the potatoes and added them to the skillet. Next, she started on the eggs.

"What can I do to help?" Mary asked, wondering how many people Mrs. Higgins was cooking for. All that food couldn't just be for the three of them.

"It's just you and Mr. Davy this morning. So would you prefer to eat in the kitchen or the dining room?"

"The kitchen please." Mary preferred it to the

dining room, which seemed too big for two people. "Aren't you joining us?"

"No, but thank you for the invite. You newlyweds need some time alone."

Mary panicked. She didn't want Mrs. Higgins to leave. Having her here would make the conversation flow easier. She might get less tongue-tied. She had always been quite shy but this was ridiculous. It seemed she lost the ability to think clearly when facing her husband. "Please join us. I'm sure Davy would say the same if he was here. Where is he?"

"Out in the barn catching up on some of the work. He'll be in shortly." Mrs. Higgins set three places at the table much to Mary's relief. She took out the silverware as the housekeeper dished up plates of breakfast.

Mary took a seat staring at the amount of food on her plate. "I don't mean to be rude, Mrs. H, but I don't think I could finish all this food."

"You need fattening up, young lady. What you been eating back in Boston? You look half starved." Mary flushed. "Oh, me and my big mouth. I didn't mean no offense but you need your strength out here."

"There was never enough food in the orphanage. The young ones were always crying. They got stomach ache from hunger."

"Let me guess. You used to share your portion."

Mary nodded, her mouth full of delicious food. "Not just me. All the older kids did it. It was easier for us to manage the hunger pains. Drinking water helped."

"Well, there is no shortage of food around here so you help yourself. Come winter you will be glad of a few extra pounds."

"Are the winters very bad?" Mary asked, more to make conversation. She had read reports of the harsh winters in old newspapers at the library in Boston.

"They are long and can be tiresome as we often get cut off from town." Davy replied, having come in just as Mary asked the question.

Mary's stomach flipped at the sound of his voice. She looked up to find him gazing at her, his eyes as bright as his smile.

"Did you sleep well?"

"Yes, thank you." She smiled back at him shyly.

Davy took a seat and smiled his thanks at the housekeeper as she put a plate piled high with food in front of him. "When we finish eating, would you like a tour of the ranch? I have to check on some of the herd and I want to start on your shooting lessons."

Drat, I hoped he had forgotten about them. She forced herself to smile, not wanting to appear stupid at being afraid of guns. "Thank you, that would be lovely."

Davy gave her a funny look at her tone but she was saved from reacting by Mrs. H.

"Should I pack you a picnic? Then you can make a day of it?" Mrs. Higgins asked.

Mary hoped he would say yes, as a picnic would be good. Maybe she could eat really slowly so they wouldn't have time for the shooting lessons. She didn't think he would like the fact she hated guns.

"You have the nicest ideas, Mrs. H. A picnic sounds great." Davy winked at Mary, causing tingles to race up and down her spine. "I will just go grab the old rifle. Mary can use it for practice."

* * *

THEY TRAVELLED in silence for a bit as Davy checked on a couple of strays from his herd.

"I thought you would have lots more cows given the size of this place." Mary looked surprised as Davy burst out laughing.

Mary shifted in the seat. Davy pointed in the distance. "The cattle graze all over the range. We don't keep them penned in."

"But how do you know which ones are yours?"

"We brand them as calves. In spring, we do a roundup where we separate out our cattle from the neighbors. If we find new calves, we brand those.

Then come fall, we round up the ones ready to go to market. We used to have to drive them for miles to the train station but now we just take them to town. The railroad ships them to the east to the slaughter houses." He noticed Mary's grimace and smiled to himself. She wasn't as hard as she made herself out to be.

CHAPTER 23

*H*e decided to lighten the mood by pointing out various things to Mary making her laugh. He loved doing it. Her whole face lit up when she giggled making it harder not to lean over and kiss her. After a while, he couldn't ignore the grumbling of his stomach any longer.

"Why don't we sit and eat?"

"Over there?" Mary pointed to a spot under a tree. "I could do with getting out of the sun for a bit."

Davy could have kicked himself. He had forgotten she wasn't used to blazing sunshine. With her coloring, she was likely to burn. Mrs. H had packed a generous lunch, which they both enjoyed. Davy liked how Mary ate with gusto. He had little time for picky eaters. A while after they had finished eating, he got up.

"Are we leaving now?"

Delighted at her reluctance to leave, Davy decided now was a good time to start her shooting lessons. "The sun has gone down a little. We can start on your lessons."

"Do we have to?" Mary busied herself with the leftovers so she didn't have to see his reaction.

"There's no need to be frightened. We'll only shoot some old cans today. I'll go set them up over there and you follow when you're ready."

YOU'LL GROW *roots and spread like a tree before I'm ready to fire a gun.* But she didn't say anything. Instead, she delayed as long as she could before following him. Mary eyed the can with trepidation. It was too far away. There was no way she would hit it. Especially with Davy standing beside her. He was distracting at the best of times but today it was worse. His hair curled along his collar. Fighting the temptation to run her fingers through it, she tried to concentrate on what he was saying. He showed her how to hold the gun, warning her yet again about the recoil. She bit her lip trying to concentrate on his words rather than his nearness.

"You ready?"

Mary stared at his mouth. She wondered what it would be like if he kissed her again.

"Mary?"

She started. "Sorry. I was…" What could she say? She wasn't about to admit to wanting a kiss. She shook her head, rubbed her hands down her skirt and took the gun out of his hands. Taking aim, she squeezed her eyes shut and pulled the trigger. The loud noise shook her whole body. It seemed to echo off the mountains. It took a few seconds for her to realize Davy was laughing. "What's so funny? You didn't really expect me to hit it, did you?"

"If you opened your eyes when taking aim, you might fare a bit better."

Mary blushed as she looked at the ground. *He must think I am an idiot.*

"Try again."

She took aim again and this time, managed to keep her eyes open but forgot about the recoil. The can sat untouched. Rubbing her shoulder, she watched as Davy demonstrated again what she should do. Over and over she tried, until she had lost count of the number of times she fired the gun. Still the can didn't move. Finally her patience gave out. She stalked down to where the can sat on the fence and shoved it off using the butt of the rifle. "There. I hit it. Can we go home now?" She stood glaring at her husband who was obviously trying his best not to laugh. His eyes were streaming as his cheeks reddened. "Don't you dare laugh at me!"

"Sorry, Mary" Davy managed to stutter before erupting with laughter. He continued to laugh for a few minutes, as she got angrier. "I am warning you, Davy Sullivan. Stop laughing this minute or I will shoot you." He stopped for a second to stare at her but the minute their eyes met, he started again. He shook his head but didn't stop. She tried hard to contain her own giggles but failed miserably. She sank to her knees in the lush green grass, tears falling down her face as she giggled.

"I am real sorry, Mary."

"You should be. A good husband doesn't laugh at his wife."

"I wasn't laughing at you, darling, but with you." He looked at her, lifting his hand to push some loose tendrils of hair out of her eyes. "Perhaps you are right. A good husband should say he is sorry. With a kiss…" He reached for her chin, rubbing his fingers tenderly along the outline of her face. His eyes never left hers as he tilted her head upwards. Leaning in, he grazed his lips across hers. Mary's lips parted as she opened up to his gentle persuasion. With a groan, he gathered her to him not breaking the kiss. His hands caressed her back wishing there wasn't any material between them. His mouth moved from her lips to kiss her face, her eyelids, and nose before moving back to her lips. She melted into his embrace, her fingers reaching up to play in his hair before moving to stroke the back of his neck.

HE SHUDDERED AT HER TOUCH. His body responded, demanding more. As the kiss deepened, she wound her hands around him pulling him closer. He pushed her gently back onto the grass easing his body weight so he didn't crush her. He didn't want to scare her with the evidence of his growing desire. He resisted the temptation to intimately caress her body sensing she had lost control. In her innocence, she had no idea of how close to the edge he was. Reluctantly, he broke their kiss ignoring her groan of disappointment, twisting so that she now lay across him, her head cradled on his shoulder. Her quickened breathing matched his. He wished they were at home. He would pick her up and take her upstairs to claim her as his wife. But their first time wouldn't be in a field. His wife deserved better.

CHAPTER 24

"I need to start working. I can't sit around all day. It isn't natural." Mary sat at the table after breakfast. Davy was working and she was bored. She wasn't used to sitting around with nothing to do. The guilt ate away at her, especially when Mrs. H never seemed to stop moving. "Please let me help, Mrs. H. I wasn't cut out to be a lady of leisure."

Mrs. Higgins laughed. "Davy was trying to ease you in gently. I think he was afraid you might leave if you knew just how hard it is here on the ranch. You might as well enjoy the rest while you can."

"Please, Mrs. H. There must be something I can do. Can you teach me how to milk the cows or maybe I can collect the eggs? I would offer to cook but I don't think Davy and the men would appreciate that."

"Don't sell yourself short, Miss Mary. There will be

plenty who will do that for you. The boys aren't too fussy. So long as the food is hot and plentiful, they are happy." Mrs. H looked at Mary for a few seconds. "If you really want to be useful, I will show you what to do tomorrow. Today I have to go into town. You can come with me and visit with Katie. You'd like that wouldn't you?"

Mary nodded.

Mrs. H drove the wagon toward town. "We grow most of the food we need. I like gardening. I am better at growing vegetables than fruit. We have canning days at the end of the summer so we can put aside food for the winter."

"What do you need from town?"

"Flour, sugar and spices. And some candy for Davy. He has a sweet tooth. What about you? Are you going to make a new dress for the festival?"

"I guess so. I don't really have anything suitable. I've never been to a harvest festival before. We have fairs in Ireland. Daddy took us a couple of times but back when we were kids."

"The festival is great fun. It's a time for everyone to take a break. The men get to blow off some steam and us women get a chance to catch up with our neighbors. There are lots of competitions, including a pie eating contest. Davy always enters that one. You wouldn't know by looking at him but he can eat a whole lot. I told Martha I would bake a load of pies for the festival. You can help me with that if you'd like."

"Thank you Mrs. H." She wanted to be useful and she liked spending time with Mrs. H. They pulled up outside the store just as Katie came out to sweep the step.

"Good morning, Mrs. H, Mary. Wasn't expecting you in town today. You got a letter from Boston, Mary. Daniel has it behind the counter."

Mary gave Katie a quick hug before running in to get her letter. She presumed it was one of the girls as Cathy didn't live in Boston anymore. She scanned the contents of the letter before sitting down with a bump.

"What's wrong, Mary?"

"Ben tried to run away. He didn't get far but the nuns beat him." She clenched her fist reading Sorcha's letter.

"Beat who?"

"Ben. He's a six year old cripple who came to live at the orphanage after Cathy left. The poor child has enough scars from the beatings his parents dished out. Oh, I wish I was in Boston."

"Come upstairs. I'll make you some tea. Mrs. H has

gone to visit a few people. She won't be back for a while."

Mary followed Katie upstairs, reading the letter as she went. "Sorcha says Ben wanted to come after me. He's only a baby, Katie, why would anyone want to give away their own child?"

Katie rubbed her belly. "I can't imagine anyone giving up their baby. Is there no chance for him to be adopted?"

"Nobody wants us orphans for the most part. Unless they want child labor. Ben wouldn't be much use in their eyes. But he is such a sweet boy, Katie." The tears stopped Mary talking. Katie held her hand until she composed herself.

"What else does Sorcha say? Did she mention Father Molloy?"

Mary smiled. The kindly old priest had been good to both Katie and Mary, allowing them time to catch up together as well as feeding them treats. "She says he comes regularly for tea with Cook and the two of them are still arguing. Here read it for yourself." Mary cradled the warm tea in her hands while Katie read the rest of Sorcha's letter.

"She wants to know if there is anyone else looking for a wife. She says life is unbearable at the orphanage. She'll be eighteen next year so will be able to leave." Katie put the letter on the table. "There's loads of single men in Clover Springs. I'm sure we can find someone." Katie started giggling.

"What's so funny?"

"Sorry, but can you imagine Mrs. Grey's face if she knows there is another Irish bride on her way to Clover Springs."

"You haven't found her a husband yet."

"But I will, if only to wind Mrs. Grey up."

Mary burst out laughing at the look on Katie's face. She missed Ben and wanted nothing more than to give him a big hug but that wasn't possible now. But maybe it could be…

CHAPTER 25

A few days later, Davy took Mary on another picnic. He knew he should be working but he couldn't help wanting to spend time with his wife.

"This is beautiful, Davy."

"It's my special thinking place. Ma said she always knew where to look for me if I went missing as a kid."

"It's so peaceful up here. You could forget about all your troubles."

"Are you not happy here, Mary? I know it's difficult with you not having family nearby. I hope in time you come to love it."

"I like it fine but I guess I do miss my family and Ben, most of all."

"Ben?" Davy's body stiffened. Was this a man she loved in Boston? "I wasn't aware I had competition."

Mary laughed. Davy loved to hear her laughing. It was infectious.

"You don't, unless you consider a six year old boy competition."

"I didn't know you had a brother." Davy was confused. He was sure Katie had said Mary's sister was the only other survivor of the trip from Ireland.

"Ben's not my brother. He lives at the orphanage. I grew very fond of him."

"Oh, another orphan."

"No, he's not. His parents are alive, or at least they were."

"What's he doing living in an orphanage then?'" He saw the pain in Mary's eyes and immediately regretted asking. "Sorry, I didn't mean to cause you upset."

"It's not you. Ben is crippled. He had polio when he was two and it left him with a damaged leg. His parents gave him to the nuns when they decided to go to Montana. Nobody will adopt him due to his leg. The other children aren't always kind and the adults… Well the less said about them the better."

"Oh, the poor boy. Not much of a future for him, is there?"

"No. I was teaching him his letters before I came out here. Sorcha wrote to me the other day about him. That's the letter I collected from town."

"The one that had you all upset?"

Mary nodded.

"It will be hard at first but he is bound to get over it. Someone else will look after him."

"Will they? Sorcha said Ben tried to run away. He told Sister Una he was going to follow me. Mother Superior had him whipped for causing upset."

Davy clenched his fist. He didn't like violence and it pained him to think of any child being beaten particularly one so young. And a cripple at that.

"People are so cruel, Davy. He is only a child. I shouldn't have left him."

Davy took her in his arms, trying to soothe her grief as she gave in to tears. She sobbed her heart out on his shoulder. "Shush, Mary. Sure, what could you do? You couldn't bring him with you?"

Mary sniffed before staring up at him. "Couldn't I? There is plenty of space around here. He wouldn't be a burden. I would take care of him."

Davy moved away from her slightly. He rubbed his jaw before saying as gently as he could. "A ranch is no place for a cripple, Mary. There are far too many things that could happen."

"Like what?"

"Don't look at me like that. You haven't seen what the winters are like out here. This isn't Boston. Everyone has to pull his or her weight on a ranch. Otherwise, they won't survive."

"You want children, don't you? You wouldn't expect your six year old son to earn his keep, would you?"

"That's different."

"Why?"

Davy struggled to contain his frustration. "Mary, you can't compare a stranger to our own child."

"He's not a stranger. Not to me."

Davy stood up, having decided it was best to return home. He didn't want to hurt Mary's feelings any more than he already had but he wasn't about to agree to her request. "Mary, we haven't been married that long. We need time to get to know each other before we take on responsibility for a child." She opened her mouth but he shook his head. "Please don't say anything else. I am very sorry, Mary, but I won't change my mind. Let's go. I have chores to do." He walked back to the horses feeling her eyes boring into his back. He swore to himself. How had such a nice afternoon ended on such a sour note?

MARY WATCHED Davy stride toward the horses. He was upset. She knew he felt sorry for Ben and couldn't really understand why he was so against bringing the child out here. Maybe it was just too soon to mention adopting Ben. As she gathered the picnic things together she went over and over what had happened. What had she been thinking? She barely knew her husband. How could she expect him to take on another man's child? Daniel took on Ellen. *That's different. He was hardly going to turn away Katie's sister. Ben wasn't her blood kin.* She wished she could turn the clock back and start their afternoon over. Their day had started with such promise too. *When am I going to learn to keep my mouth shut?*

When she had everything packed up, she walked over to where Davy stood waiting. She smiled before she realized he wasn't looking at her. "Davy, I'm sorry. I shouldn't have said anything about Ben."

"Don't worry about it." Davy took the basket from her and put it in the wagon. He held out his hand to help her onto the seat. Her skin shivered at the contact. She looked into his eyes and saw he felt the attraction, too. On impulse, she leaned forward and kissed his cheek. "Thank you for taking me to see your special place. I hope we can have a longer picnic next time."

They rode home in silence. Mary thought it was better to let Davy get over the upset in his own time. She remembered her mam saying men needed time to come to a decision. Maybe the silence meant he was thinking it over.

CHAPTER 26

Mary sat and poured coffee for both of them. She resolved to buy some tea when she next went to the store. She then filled her plate with bacon, eggs and biscuits. Mrs. H was a wonderful cook and the fresh food tasted so much better than the food in Boston. Davy came in just as she was finished. Mrs. H set a plate of food on the table as he washed his hands.

"Sorry if I disturbed you this morning. I had to get an early start." Davy smiled at Mary.

Her heart thumping she smiled back although she could feel her cheeks turning pink. "I was just asking Mrs. H to show me how I can help. It doesn't feel right to stay in bed when you work so hard."

Davy nodded his eyes full of approval but as his mouth was full he didn't say anything. Mary turned to the housekeeper. "What would you like me to start on today? Perhaps I could help with the laundry."

Mrs. H shook her head. "We will leave that to another morning. Let's go see if the hens have lain this morning. I usually do it before breakfast but didn't get a chance this morning."

Mary smiled. How hard could it be to collect eggs? She soon changed her mind after the third painful peck on her hands. "Ouch. You nasty little bird."

Mrs. H stood with her hands on her hips laughing loudly. "Sorry, Miss Mary, but you should see your face. You look like you would put poor old Agnes in the crock pot for dinner."

"Agnes? You name all the hens?"

"Sure do. They are nice creatures. You just need to know how to handle them. See like this."

Mary stared as the housekeeper collected three eggs without being threatened, never mind pecked.

"Don't worry, they will get used to you soon enough."

"Do you keep all the eggs or does Davy sell some?"

"We take some to the store if he is going into town but usually we keep them for the ranch. The men appreciate the cakes I make. Keeps them sweet when the weather turns nasty. It's a hard life working outdoors especially when the cold season comes." Mrs. H handed the basket now full of eggs to Mary.

"Tomorrow you can do this while I'm making break-fast. Have you ever milked a cow?"

"Once and she didn't kick so that's good, isn't it?"

Mrs. H laughed before taking Mary's arm and showing her where the cows lived. "One of the boys currently looks after the cows but it would help if you could take over. It could do with a woman's touch, couldn't it?" Mary looked around the barn nodding in agreement. The hay looked like it hadn't been turned as often as it could. The cows weren't too clean either. "Jeb knows better than to try to milk dirty cows. He will make us all ill." Mrs. H tutted, not hiding her disapproval.

"Who is Jeb?"

"One of the youngsters. His Pa works for Davy. His Ma is sick and Davy thought he could help the family out a little more if the youngsters earned a few coins. Jeb isn't cut out for farming. He likes reading and such. He should be in school really."

"What age is he?"

"Not rightly sure. About nine I would guess, although he could be small for his age. Doesn't say much. Always has his nose stuck in a book. Seen his Pa hit him more than once for not doing his chores."

Mary's heart went out to the little boy she had yet to meet. She resolved to help him get to school. Handing the basket back to Mrs. H, she rolled her sleeves up. She mightn't know much about ranching but she was an expert on cleaning. In no time, this barn would shine. Of that, she was determined. Mrs. H went back to the house leaving Mary to it. She worked for a while before realizing someone was watching her. She looked up to find a boy dressed more or less in rags. He didn't look much cleaner than the barn and sported an ugly looking black eye.

"Why you working here?"

"I thought I would help you get the barn sorted. It needs a good clean. I take it you're Jeb?"

"Who's asking?"

Surprised at his cheek, Mary didn't get a chance to answer. Instead a voice came from behind her.

"The lady is my wife, young man."

Jeb paled under his freckles. "Sorry, Boss." He mumbled kicking at the straw with his foot.

Mary put her hand on Davy's arm to thank him for his support before focusing on the youngster. "You weren't to know, Jeb. We haven't had a chance to be introduced properly. My name is Mary and I need your help. It's my first time in a barn. I am relying on you to show me what needs to be done."

"Your first time in a barn? Where you been up to now?"

"I came from a small village in Ireland and then

lived in Boston for a while. They don't have much call for barns in a city."

"What's it like living in a city?"

Mary smiled at the wistful look on the child's face. "It's very different out here. For a start, you can't often see the stars, as there are lots of buildings blocking your view. There are lots of people too, so the streets get very crowded. When you are all grown up, you can go visit Boston and other places."

"That will take forever. I want to go now."

"Mrs. Higgins says you like to read. I brought a couple of books with me. What say we have a look at them later?"

"I got chores to do."

"I'll make a deal with you. If you show me what to do in the barn, then I will help you with your chores. When we are finished, we will ask Mrs. Higgins for some cookies and go look at the books."

"For real?"

Mary watched his face, distrust fighting with hope. "Yes it's for real. Now let's get to work."

CHAPTER 27

They were so engrossed in their chat and the subsequent chores; neither noticed Davy leave the barn. Mary seemed happier this morning. He had got little sleep last night. His mind kept going over and over their conversation. He hadn't changed his mind. It was too soon to bring someone else into their relationship even if it was a child. He liked children and hated to think of anyone mistreating one, especially a cripple. But life was hard on the ranch. It was better if Ben stayed in Boston.

Maybe Jeb would help Mary forget about her past. He had to admit his wife had a real way with children. She had gotten Jeb to trust her, no mean feat considering how the child had been treated in the past. It wasn't his fault his Pa was a drunk and a wife beater but some of the townsfolk seemed to think the boy would grow up just like Rowdy. Davy clenched his hands. He would love to give Rowdy a black eye but knew anything he dished out to the father would have repercussions for the whole family. It galled him that he couldn't stop the man from beating up his wife and children. The law wouldn't intervene either although Davy believed the Sheriff wished he could. He didn't know how long he could keep Rowdy on the payroll. The other lads were sick of his drunken binges and most didn't appreciate the way he treated his family. But if he sacked him, the family would be destitute and he couldn't have that on his conscious. He must remind Mrs. H to put some salve in the next food basket she sent to the Brown's shack. It might take the sting out of Jeb's bruises.

Davy hopped onto his horse and let the animal gallop off toward the range. Mary was an asset to the ranch, no doubt about that. He wished he could spend all day helping her and Jeb in the barn but there wasn't time. He had to keep on top of the jobs while the weather held. He looked up at the sky wondering how long the unseasonably warm weather would last. Then he heard gunshots. They were coming from the area where his men had been working yesterday. Digging his heels in, he galloped toward the gunfire, one hand on his gun. Thankfully, all his men were safe but there was a wounded stranger on the ground.

"Who is it?"

"Don't know boss. He passed out but he'll live. Haven't seen him around. What do you want to do? Go after them?"

Davy was torn. "Any of you see where they went? How many were there?"

"Reckon three, boss, but it's hard to know if they were alone or part of the larger gang some of the other ranchers been complaining about."

Davy stared into the distance. Should he head after them or wait for the sheriff. What if it was a ruse to get them all away from the ranch? Mary? He couldn't leave her without protection. Especially since she hadn't taken so well to her shooting lessons. "Best leave it to the sheriff. He will want to talk to you. He may recognize this dirt bag." The stranger groaned. "Tie him up, Henry. We don't want him getting away."

Davy watched as Henry tied up the cowboy none too gently. He was younger than he expected but it was pointless feeling sorry for him. Cattle rustling was a serious crime. Everyone knew the penalty. "Henry, you take a couple of the boys and take our friend here to town." Henry nodded before mounting his horse. "Not a word of this at the ranch okay. I don't want my wife spooked. All right you lads, get those cattle rounded up. We will move them closer to the ranch for now. I want to know as soon as possible how many we lost." Davy sighed heavily. The last thing they needed was to lose cattle to rustlers. "Henry come find me when you get back. We need to double the watch for the time being."

"Sure thing, boss." Henry rode off with the now conscious rustler tied to the saddle of his horse. The rest of them rounded up the cattle. Davy thanked the Lord his men had disturbed the rustlers and yet escaped unharmed. They had only lost a few steer, nothing compared to what could have happened.

After he washed up, he headed into the ranch house. Mrs. H was in the kitchen.

"I sent Miss Mary up for a nap. The poor girl has that barn looking so clean you could eat your dinner off the floor." Mrs. H looked up when silence met her words. "Cat got your tongue?"

"Mrs. H, you need to stay close to the house for the next few days. Make sure Mary doesn't go far, too. The men disturbed some rustlers. They seem to have gone now but I can't be sure. Henry took one of them to the Sheriff. I'm going into town to find out what's going on. I don't want you telling Mary what happened. No point in scaring her."

"I won't say a word."

CHAPTER 28

*M*ary looked up from the hem she was sewing. She was working on Ellen's harvest festival dress while Katie cut out Mary's dress. "Katie, do you mind if I ask you something?"

"Of course not."

"Do you ever find Daniel is, well he's a little over-protective?"

"My Daniel? Whatever makes you think that? The fact he acts like I am the first woman ever to fall pregnant?"

"Oh no, I didn't notice anything. I just wondered." Mary blushed. She couldn't believe Katie thought she had just criticized Daniel.

"Relax, Mary. I know you didn't mean anything bad. Is Davy the same?"

"Well, I am not pregnant, so I guess not." The two

women laughed. With Katie looking at her intently, Mary knew she had to say something. "Sometimes Davy can get a little out of sorts. Like if a man says good morning or something like that. They don't mean to be anything other than mannerly. But Davy, well..." Guilt made Mary stop. Katie may be her friend but Davy was her husband.

"Davy gets jealous. All men are a bit like that especially with a new wife in a town full of single men. He is probably worrying you might run off with someone rich and handsome.

"My Davy is handsome." Mary's hand flew to her mouth as her cheeks burned.

Katie grinned. "Yes, he is. You're quite taken with your new husband. I am so glad. I was a little worried after he turned up smelling so bad."

Mary smiled. "He smells okay now." She burned up at the teasing glance Katie gave her. "I do like him, Katie, but he seems to, well it's almost as if he really doesn't trust me. I can't talk to anyone without him asking me lots of questions about what we were talking about. The other day he seemed annoyed when I laughed at a joke Henry made. It makes me uneasy."

"Have you tried speaking to Davy?"

"No, what do I say? I can't exactly ask him if he's jealous."

"No, not outright, but you can make an effort to make him feel more comfortable about you two."

"You think he might feel a bit strange?"

"You may be married but, really, you are both still strangers. You need to get to know one another and with time, love and trust will grow."

"You're probably right." Mary didn't want to discuss it anymore. "How are you feeling? Is the baby kicking yet?"

"Oh yes, especially at night. I think it will be a boy. He never seems to want to sit still." Katie smiled, her face lit up with a serene glow. "Coming to Clover Springs was the best decision I ever made. It will be the same for you Mary. Just give it time."

MARY WALKED BACK toward the livery stables to meet Davy. She was so caught up in thinking about her husband she didn't see the man in front of her until it was too late. They collided and Mary would have fallen over if the man hadn't grabbed her arm. He held onto her for a few seconds before the two of them sprung apart.

"Excuse me Ma'am. I wasn't looking where I was going. Are you all right?" The man took his hat off and held it in his hands, his concerned eyes looking down at her.

Mary nodded although she felt rather faint. "It was my fault. I wasn't paying attention. I am sorry Mr...." She couldn't remember his name. He didn't look familiar but she had met so many new people in the last few days, that didn't mean a lot.

"Mary, what's wrong. Is this man annoying you?"

Mary's heart fell at the irate sound of her husband's voice. How long had he been standing there? Why did she feel guilty? It was an accident. "Davy, this man saved me from falling onto the street. I was away with the fairies and walked straight into him."

"No, ma'am, the fault was mine. I should have been paying closer attention." At Davy's cough, the man turned redder and started walking faster. "Good day, Ma'am."

Mary rounded on Davy. "What are you glaring at?"

"Why should I be upset?" His sarcastic tone didn't help Mary get control of her temper. "A strange man had his hands on my wife and she seems to think I'm the one with the problem."

"You are." She was glad her words struck home, if the surprised look on his face was anything to go by. "The gentleman held me so I didn't fall. If he hadn't put his hand on me, I would be sitting in the street. Perhaps you would have preferred that."

CHAPTER 29

$\mathcal{M}$ary stormed off down the street. She couldn't bear to look at Davy now and given her temper, she might say something she would live to regret. Honestly, what did the man think she was going to do? If he couldn't trust her to walk down the main street in town, how could he expect her to live out in the middle of nowhere surrounded by ranch hands? She tried to calm down but every time she thought of the way he had looked at her, her temper rose again. She had walked about a mile before she heard the wagon behind her.

"Do you intend walking the whole way home?"

Mary ignored Davy and kept walking.

"Mary, I'm sorry. I didn't know he was trying to help. When I saw him with his hands on you…"

"You decided I was wanton."

"Not you, Mary."

Mary rounded on him, her hands on her hips and her eyes blazing. "Who then? Who else are you married to? I have never been so embarrassed in all my life. I know we are strangers but you implied I would behave in a less than respectable manner with someone I just met. In the middle of a street. Whatever got into you, Davy Sullivan?"

He jumped down from the wagon and stood in front of her. Her temper cooled at the look in his eyes but she couldn't let this go.

"I apologize. I behaved badly."

"Yes, you did."

"It's only because I care."

"Funny way of showing it. If someone saw the way you reacted, my reputation would be mud in this town. Isn't it bad enough they all know I was desperate without you making out I am wanton, too." She brushed the tears away angrily. She always cried when she was angry.

He reached out using the tip of his finger to wipe away the tears. Her breath shuddered as she tried to breathe deeper. His closeness was having an effect on her, making it difficult to concentrate. "Please don't cry. I said I was sorry."

"Davy, what makes you behave like this? I am your wife. For better or worse." He put his hands in his pockets, looking at the dirt road. She let the silence go on for a few moments. "Davy, you have to trust me. I don't know why you act the way you do. Someday I hope you will tell me." She waited for a reply but none was forthcoming. She sighed. Katie had said she would need patience. She held out her hand. "We can't stand around all day. There's work to be done. Can you help me into the wagon, please? I want to go home."

"With me?"

"Of course with you. I may still be real annoyed with you but I'm stuck with you. You're my husband."

Davy gave her a tentative smile before helping her into the wagon. He sat up beside her. They rode along in silence for a while. Mary stole a few glances at her husband but his face was inscrutable. She wondered what he was thinking about but now was not the time to ask.

CHAPTER 30

*D*avy knew Mary was looking at him, trying to work out what was the matter. He couldn't tell her. He had missed her when she visited with Katie. It was only a couple of hours but it felt like days. It was hard to believe that the woman had only been a part of his life for a week. He was behaving like a love struck boy. Love! Where had that come from? He didn't love her. He barely knew her. She had a real fiery temper though. His body hardened at the thought of her passionate nature. He shifted uncomfortably in the wagon seat. Think of the cold creek.

He should have thought of a cold swim when he had come out of the livery to see a man with his hand on Mary's arm. Instead, he had let the redness descend and behaved badly. He didn't blame his wife for being sore with him. He deserved it. She was right. He had made a scene and put both their reputations at risk. All the man had done was save Mary from a potentially nasty fall.

He had to get this jealousy under control or he would lose everything. He stole a glance at his wife. She was so different to Tilly. She didn't look like her physically but it wasn't just that. She was more circumspect around people. Tilly had been a young girl who had too much freedom. Her father and uncle hadn't given her any real teaching on how to deal with society and its expectations.

He cleared his throat desperate to break the silence that had built up between them. He didn't know what to say. He could apologize again but how often did he need to say he was sorry. He could promise not to react like that again but that wasn't one he was likely to be able to keep. Maybe he could speak to Reverend Tim about his demons.

"Is this all your land?" Mary asked looking around her.

Surprised at her question, Davy replied. "It's our land." Pleased by the smile she gave him and relieved she seemed to have forgiven him, he pointed out different landmarks to her as they drove home. His wife may not have much ranching experience but she was intelligent. Her questions were thoughtful. The rest of the journey passed pleasantly and soon they were in sight of the house. He stopped the wagon and turned to face her. Taking her hands in his, he said, "I'm sorry for what happened in town. I have a lot to learn about being married."

"We will learn together."

He leaned in to give her a kiss on the cheek but she moved at the last minute. His lips met hers. Groaning, he pulled her closer toward him as the kiss deepened. Her lips were pliant beneath his, her innocence intoxicating. Then he heard the barn door bang. Someone was letting them know they were being watched. Regretfully he released his wife, her eyes still shut, her face red from passion. He kissed the tip for her nose. "Best get back to the house."

She nodded but didn't move away from his side. Keeping one arm around her, he clicked the reins and the wagon moved forward. When they reached the barn, he jumped down and walked round to help Mary. Putting his hands around her tiny waist, he swung her down not releasing her immediately. He liked the feel of her body close to his. He bent to graze his lips across her forehead.

MARY WAS glad he held her close. She didn't trust her legs to move properly. The kiss had been so fine; her body still reeled from the sensations that had flooded her. He must care for her but then kisses meant different things to men. Didn't they? He let her go, moving around the back of the wagon to unload the supplies they had brought home. Mrs. Higgins came out of the door just at that moment preventing any further intimacy.

"Are you feeling all right, Miss Mary? Your cheeks are rather flushed."

Mary blushed even more as she heard Davy try to smother a laugh behind her.

ary sat in the kitchen sewing as Mrs. H baked some cakes. Davy came in briefly and stole some cookies on his way out.

"I can't believe it's his twenty fifth birthday next month. It only seems like yesterday he was a boy following his Pa everywhere."

"It's Davy's birthday? Which day?" Mary asked feeling more than a little embarrassed. She didn't know her own husband's birthday.

"Tuesday the 20th. Now take that look off your face. You got plenty of time to make him something nice. A new shirt would come in useful. I think he feeds his to the animals. There's that many holes in them, something must be chewing on it."

"I'd like to get him something special. He's been so

good to me buying me lots of new things. Maybe I could buy him something just for himself?"

"I don't expect he shares his shirts with the ranch hands."

"It's not very romantic though, is it? I can sew him a shirt anytime."

Mrs. Higgins looked her up and down. "Would you be trying to court your husband, Miss Mary?" She grinned as the redness spread up Mary's neck and cheeks.

"Oh it's been so long since I felt like that. I remember when my Tom took me to see our first home. We'd been living with his folks until then. Right old battle-axe his mother was. You mark my words. I thought I had gone to heaven when he carried me through the door of our little cabin. Only had one room really but to me it was a palace."

"I can't get him a cabin, Mrs. H, but there must be something."

"What about a new saddle?"

"I'm not sure I can afford one of those. Aren't they expensive."

"Yes they are but it so happens that one of the ranch hands won a saddle in a poker game. He won a few different things including the other man's gun. Anyhow, he has a saddle and was griping the other day he would prefer hard cash. You might be able to do a deal with him."

"Could you do it, Mrs. H? Please. I don't feel too comfortable around the men. Davy ..." Mary stopped, afraid she had said too much.

"Davy doesn't like you spending too much time with them. Understandable, I guess, given what happened."

"What do you mean?" Mary's curiosity was peaked but a guarded look came over Mrs. Higgins face.

"Land sakes, girl. What do you mean what happened? You got married, remember. Davy, being the boss, doesn't want the men being familiar with his wife. They are good boys really but they don't get to mix too much with the opposite sex. Makes them a bit rough around the edges. Davy must be worried they might say something to upset you. Not on purpose like but because they just don't know better." Mrs. Higgins paused for breath. "How did I get to lollygagging? Oh yes, the saddle. I'll have a word with Mick. He'll be glad to get rid of it, I reckon."

"Thanks, Mrs. H, I don't know what I'd do without you."

CHAPTER 32

*D*avy held the door of the store open for a customer. He had called to collect Mary who was visiting with Katie. He couldn't see his wife but there were quite a few customers in the store. Daniel was behind the counter.

"Yes, he married an Irish girl, too. Another one of those so-called mail order brides. Why would any decent girl come out west to marry a stranger?"

"Maybe they didn't have a choice?"

"More like they had reason to leave Boston. There are decent men out East too, aren't there? No, you mark my words, no respectable woman is going to travel miles out west. And without a chaperone too? I am surprised at Martha Sullivan. I thought she would have higher standards."

"Well, I guess there weren't any suitable single

ladies in Clover Springs." Mrs. Shaw examined a piece of cloth putting it back with a sigh of regret. Everyone knew her husband drank more than he earned but she tried her best to keep up appearances. Unfortunately she hung on every word Mrs. Grey said, perhaps in the hope that having rich friends kept her respectable.

"The town has one or two well refined young ladies. A couple are due back from school shortly."

"Like your niece, Mrs. Grey?"

"Oh, Mr. Sullivan, I didn't see you there." Mrs. Grey looked Davy up and down, not hiding her disdain at his dirty clothes.

"Obviously." Davy clenched his fists discretely as he tried to get his temper under control. He wouldn't do the Sullivan name any good by losing his temper with this cantankerous old biddy.

"Mrs. Grey was just telling me all about your wedding. My congratulations." Mrs. Shaw nodded to Davy, her ears pink with embarrassment. She made a show of looking at the clock. "Oh, is that the time? I must go. Mr. Shaw will want his dinner. Goodbye, Mrs. Grey, Mr. Sullivan." Davy watched as the older woman almost tripped over her own feet in her haste to get out the store door. He saw Daniel raise his eyebrow but instead turned his attention to Mrs. Grey. The old bat didn't even have the grace to look embarrassed. She sniffed before turning her attention back to Daniel. "Please see that my list is filled and sent out to the house. I don't have time to wait any longer."

Davy watched open mouthed as the woman didn't wait for Daniel to answer but marched out the store door. "I will swing for that woman one day." He said to his brother through clenched teeth.

"I think you might have to get in line. That woman has a way of getting everyone's backs up. She only has to look at someone to upset them." Daniel served another customer who nodded their agreement. Davy waited till the store had quieted down. "How's Katie doing?"

A worried look came into Daniel's eyes. "Ma and Mary are with her. She keeps having pains but the doctor says it's too early. Ma insisted she rest more. Mary is up there reading to her. Katie finds it difficult to sit still for very long."

Davy nodded knowing just how much his sister in law liked to keep busy. It wasn't in her nature to sit around letting others do her chores. He hoped she would listen to reason. Having a baby was the most natural thing in the world but it was still a dangerous time. There was more than one man in Clover Springs who had lost his wife in childbirth. Thinking like that didn't help anyone. "What can I do to help? There must be something you need?"

"Thanks, big brother, but there is nothing. Mary

brought some food from Mrs. H. She baked fresh biscuits earlier. Ma and Ellen saw to the rest of the chores. The only job I have to do is deliver these items to Mrs. Grey. "

"I can take them." Davy didn't realize he was speaking until the words were out.

Daniel looked down at the list in front of him before grinning up at his brother. "No offense but you are the last person I would send on this job."

"Happens you're right. That woman makes me mad."

"You don't say." The two brothers burst out laughing causing a smile to appear on their Ma's face as she walked in from the back.

"You two feeling all right out here?"

"Yes, Ma. How's my wife?" Daniel asked, giving his Ma a kiss on the cheek.

She reached up to hold his face in her hands before kissing him lightly on the cheek. "She is doing well, son. You keep out of her way and let her rest. She needs her strength."

"Yes, Ma."

"Davy, thank goodness you are here. I need some help with the festival."

"Sorry, Ma, but I got…"

"David Sullivan, I haven't got time to listen to excuses. There's work to be done. Reverend Timmons is depending on us. Katie made a list of things she wants us to do. Come on. The tables aren't going to set up themselves."

"Yes, Ma." Davy threw his eyes up to heaven before grinning at his brother. He followed his mother out of the store. He knew better than to argue with her once she got a bee in her bonnet.

CHAPTER 33

*M*ary woke the morning of the harvest festival. The sun was shining. Jumping out of bed, she threw on a dress before racing downstairs to the kitchen.

"Miss Mary, where's the fire?" Mrs. H jumped as Mary came bursting into the kitchen. "Sorry, Mrs. H, I'm just excited. I've never been to a festival before. Katie made me a new dress. It's gorgeous. I hope Davy will like it. I can't wait to see all the contests and the dancing and... Oh everything."

Mrs. H's smile brightened up her whole face. "You are a tonic, Miss Mary."

"What can I do to help?" Mary moved toward the dishes. "I can wash up. You have to come with us. There is no way you are missing out on the fun. Davy insisted."

"Did I?" Davy joked from the table where he had been sitting the whole time.

Shivers ran down Mary's spine at the sound of his voice. She put her hand to her mouth as she turned around. "I thought you were outside doing chores."

He grinned before rising. "They are all done." Taking a last bite of his breakfast, he twirled her around the floor. "I am looking forward to dancing with my wife tonight, Mrs. Sullivan." He kissed her lightly on the cheek before bowing and leaving the kitchen calling, "I'll hitch up the horses. Hurry up now, we don't want to miss anything."

Mary stood, her fingers moving to the spot of his kiss. She couldn't wait to feel his arms around her later. Maybe he would kiss her thoroughly.

"Come on, Mrs. Sullivan. You best get dressed properly or he will leave without you." Mrs. H laughed as Mary gasped. Grabbing her skirts, she ran toward the stairs. He wouldn't leave without her, would he?

MAM, *thank you*. Katie offered up the silent prayer as she looked around her. Judging from the wide smiles on people's faces, everyone was having a great time. The combination of good weather, delicious food and great music meant even Mrs. Grey of all people had a smile on her face.

"It's so exciting, isn't it?" Katie poked Ellen in the side when her sister didn't answer.

"Ouch. What did you do that for?"

"Stop staring. You don't want to tell the whole town you like Johnny."

Ellen's cheeks flushed making her look younger. "Was I that obvious?"

Katie put her arm around the younger girl's shoulders. "You look good enough to eat. He needs glasses if he doesn't ask you to dance."

"Who needs glasses?"

"Never mind. It's ladies talk. Have you not eaten enough?" Katie eyed her husband's plate.

"I need to keep my strength up. I'm having a baby, don't you know."

"Today, I wish you were having it, not me." Katie smoothed her hand over her stomach.

"Are you tired? Why don't you go home?" Daniel handed the plate to Ellen. "Come on. I'll walk you back."

Katie sighed. She didn't want to miss the party but she didn't want to make a spectacle of herself either.

"Go on Sis, you are looking a bit peaky. Don't worry about me. Mary is over there."

Katie pulled her shawl tighter before giving her

sister a quick hug. "I hope you get to dance." Turning to Daniel, she took his arm and together they walked slowly back to their home.

"It was a very good day, Katie. You, Ma and the other women excelled yourselves. I can't wait to see Petersen's face tomorrow. He didn't believe anyone would beat him, let alone a storekeeper."

"He didn't seem that upset. He's a nice man."

"Really, Mrs. Sullivan, tell me more."

Katie tapped her husband's elbow. "You know I am a one man woman. I just feel sorry for Mr. Petersen. Losing his wife and boy in the floods last year was dreadful. I know he does his best. Jenny is a lovely little girl but she needs a mother."

"Are you matchmaking, my dear?"

Katie grinned. "Maybe just a little bit. Mary's friend, Sorcha, may be just a little young to take on a child. I wonder if Mrs. Gantley has anyone interested in coming to Clover Springs?"

"Before you go writing to her, you need to speak to Petersen first. He might not take kindly to your interfering."

"I don't think he will mind. I am very persuasive when I need to be."

Daniel burst out laughing. "I feel sorry for him already. He will be married before he knows what hit him."

Katie tried to smile back but couldn't stop the groan of pain. *Dear Lord. No. It's too early.*

Daniel took one look at her face and lifted her into his arms and ran for home. He put her lying on the bed.

"Daniel, don't leave me please."

Terror engulfed Katie, the pain was so severe.

"I'll get Ma and the Doc. I'll be back before you know it. Don't you dare move off that bed."

KATIE PRAYED FERVENTLY. The seconds ticked by, the pains getting worse. *Daniel, where are you?* Finally, she heard noises on the stairs. Mary and Ma arrived. Mary took her hand while Ma examined her.

"Mary, go down and start boiling some water. The doctor will need it."

"Ma, it's too soon. The baby can't come now."

"Stop fretting, Katie Sullivan." Ma's tone was sharper than usual.

Katie caught the glance Mary threw at their mother in law but another pain gripped her. She groaned again. Where was Daniel?

CHAPTER 34

*D*aniel paced up and down outside the mercantile. Davy stood watching him, powerless to do anything to help his little brother. Katie's screams had mercifully stopped but the silence was worse. How much longer would it take? "I can't lose her Davy." Daniel wiped a tear from his face before he recommenced his pacing.

"Stop thinking that way. She will be fine and so will your baby."

"You heard what the doctor said. He doesn't think he can save both of them. I want my wife to live. This is all my fault."

"That's bull. You both wanted a family. Katie is a strong woman, stubborn too. She is not going to let you bring up a child on your own. Nobody in their right mind would trust you to look after a kid."

"What was that?"

They both turned toward the store as a baby's wail rent the air. They ran in the door to see Ma coming down the stairs holding a bundle. "You got a little girl, son." She said offering the child to Daniel.

"How's Katie?"

Ma paled and appeared to struggle to speak. "Pray son. She gave everything she had to get her daughter born. She is very weak." Ma looked down at the bundle she was carrying.

Daniel didn't even look at the child. "Ma, keep the baby or give it to Davy. I am going in to my wife."

"But Doc doesn't…"

"Doc can go to blazes. I need to see Katie." He took the stairs two at a time and burst through the door of the bedroom

"Daniel, your wife needs quiet. It's all we can do for her now."

Daniel ignored the doctor. He sat on a chair near the bed and took his wife's hand. "Katie, don't you dare leave me. I won't let you go. You have a daughter downstairs who needs a Ma."

"Mr. Sullivan, that's hardly …"

"Get out of here Doc. I want to be alone with my wife." Daniel turned back to Katie. "Come on darling. I need you. Please." Daniel prayed harder than he had ever done before. Katie didn't respond no matter what he did. He tried shouting, begging, crying and simply staring but she just lay there. At some point, his ma came into the room.

"Daniel, son, take a break and meet your daughter."

"No. I'm staying with Katie."

"That little girl needs you."

"She's the reason my wife is dying."

"Daniel Sullivan. What would Katie say if she heard you? That girl did everything she could to make sure your daughter was born healthy. Don't you dare make her sacrifice be in vain."

"Stop it, Ma. You are talking as if she were dead. She's not going to die. She can't."

Martha kissed Katie's forehead. "I love you Katie Sullivan as much as I would my own child. Thank you for my granddaughter." With tears streaming down her face, she walked out of the room.

Ellen came to visit but was so upset, Davy had to support her leaving the room. Mary kissed her friend goodbye. She patted Daniel's shoulder as she left but he didn't look up. Reverend Tim also came in and said some prayers. Katie didn't even flutter an eyelid. "I will pray for you too, Daniel. Let me know if there is anything I can do." Daniel nodded, his eyes focused on Katie's face willing for a sign to show she had heard the different voices. Nothing. Daniel lay on the bed, cradling his wife. Her breathing was so shallow. It grew darker outside. "Katie darling, do you remember what we promised. You weren't ever going to leave me? I need you. I can't live without you. Can you hear me? Squeeze my hand. Please." He stared at his hand in hers, willing it to feel something. The tears started flowing as he pulled her closer and wept.

CHAPTER 35

"It's bad, Ma, isn't it?"

Ma nodded, her eyes full of tears. "Doctor reckons Katie won't pull through"

Davy swallowed. It was rare for Ma to succumb to tears. "What can I do?"

"Pray son. That's all any of us can do." Ma took Davy's arm as they walked toward the boarding house. "Mary said she would look after the boarding house while I stay with Daniel and the baby. That all right with you, son?"

"Yes, Ma, but wouldn't Mary prefer to stay with her friend?"

"Likely she would but she is more help if she looks after the guests. Mary hasn't any experience of childbirth. Doc said it would be better for me to stay close."

Davy nodded, not able to answer. He couldn't even

begin to think of how Daniel would cope if anything happened to Katie. They may have met by chance but she meant everything to his little brother. Once Ma had checked everything was in order, Davy carried her small bag back to the store. "Mary, do you want to go home to pack your things or should Mrs. H pack a bag for you?"

"No, I will come home with you if that's all right."

Davy nodded. "I will be downstairs. Take your time."

Soon they headed out to the ranch. Mary was very quiet.

"She will be fine. Katie is a fighter."

Mary nodded but remained silent. Davy moved closer to her and put his arm around her shoulders. He wanted to reassure her but the words failed him. Instead, he kept hold of her with one hand as he guided the wagon home. She didn't take long to pack her things before they were heading back to town once more.

"I will stay with you at Ma's tonight but tomorrow I have to get back to the ranch. Will you be all right?"

"I have to be. Ellen is upset and your Ma is worried too. She tries to hide it but it's obvious." Mary played with her fingers. "I just hope Katie gets better."

"She will." Davy spoke with a reassurance he didn't feel. *Dear Lord, look after them all.*

CHAPTER 36

Working at the boarding house was hard work but Mary was glad of the distraction. She cooked and cleaned all day long. She helped a little with the baby but Ma liked to keep her near the new mother. She hoped the baby's cries would reach Katie and give her the will to live. She watched the store to give Ma a break.

Ellen helped some when the school day was over. She also delivered goods for the store. It seemed she had struck up a secret friendship with Mrs. Grey. Nobody in town spent time with the woman unless they had to but Ellen had taken to visiting her regularly. She said the older woman was lonely and if she was spending time with her, she couldn't dwell on Katie.

A couple of days after Katie had given birth, there

was still no change in her condition. The doctor had said there was nothing further he could do. Mary prayed night and day for Katie and Daniel. Her brother-in-law wouldn't leave his wife's bedside. He still hadn't named their daughter. This morning, Ma was looking after the baby so Mary was taking a turn watching the store.

Mary looked up as the door opened. She smiled at Ellen, who walked in first, followed by an older woman. *Oh, that's all we need.* Plastering a smile on her face, she greeted Mrs. Grey. The woman nodded in response before closing the door behind her.

"How is Mrs. Sullivan?"

Mary stared at Ellen first and then at the other woman. What was it to her? She hadn't given Katie the time of day since she arrived in Clover Springs.

"Cat got your tongue, young woman? I asked you a question. Ellen said she was sleeping all the time."

"Still the same." Mary stuttered as the older woman fixed her with a piercing gaze.

"Well, that just won't do at all. What does the doctor say?"

"He said there wasn't anything else he could do."

"That is just typical of old sawbones. There is always something we can do. Where's the baby?"

"Martha has her. Daniel didn't want the child to waken Katie."

"Stuff and nonsense. That is exactly what she needs. Ellen, go bring the baby here. Now."

Ellen nodded before departing for the boarding house. Mrs. Grey walked toward the living quarters at the back of the store, removing her coat and gloves.

"Make some tea, girl, and something for Mrs. Sullivan to eat. Some broth would be good."

"Eat but she…"

"Don't stand around arguing with me. We don't have time to waste."

With that, Mrs. Grey was gone, leaving Mary staring after her. Reverend Timmons said God worked in mysterious ways. Maybe this is what he meant. She went back to put the closed sign on the store door before heading toward the kitchen.

CHAPTER 37

*D*aniel didn't look up as the bedroom door opened.

"Go away."

"Self-pity never got anyone anywhere, Mr. Sullivan. Your wife needs your strength. Now, open the curtains and get some air into this room."

Daniel stared open-mouthed at Mrs. Grey. "What in blazes are you doing?"

"Mind your manners, young man." Mrs. Grey lifted Katie's arm, found her pulse and started to count. A small smile lifted the edges of her mouth. Daniel pinched himself convinced he was dreaming. He watched as Mrs. Grey turned toward the door. Ellen came in carrying a bundle followed closely by his ma.

"Ellen, good girl. Bring the babe in here. Come on,

don't be afraid. Martha get me some tea and some broth. That girl downstairs hasn't brought it up yet."

Daniel watched in shock as his Ma nodded and went out again. Mrs. Grey took the bundle from Ellen's shaking hands before turning toward Katie's sleeping form.

"Kathleen Sullivan, wake up this minute. This poor child needs her mother. Typical of you Irish to be lying around when there is work to be done."

"Mrs. Grey, that's enough. Get out of here. Leave my wife be."

"I haven't started yet. Now do us all a favor and either shut up or leave." Mrs. Grey turned back toward Katie. She pinched the baby causing her to protest loudly. "Baby needs her Mama. Do you hear me, Katie Sullivan. You better wake up now or I will take your baby home and raise her myself."

Daniel took a step toward the older woman but Ellen stopped him. "Let her try, Daniel. She was a nurse in the war. She knows what she's doing."

Daniel looked between Ellen and Mrs. Grey. A nurse? How come nobody else knew that? He watched as Mrs. Grey took Katie's arms and held them around the baby. His daughter immediately edged closer to his wife's body.

"Come on, Katie, wake up now. Your baby needs her mama."

Daniel couldn't take anymore. "Stop that now, Mrs. Grey. Can't you see Katie isn't going to wake up?"

Mrs. Grey ignored him. Instead she took off the baby's clothes, leaving her naked. She then loosened Katie's nightgown before pushing the baby against her mother's skin. "Katie, your baby needs you. Fight for her. Where's that Irish spirit?"

Daniel watched in amazement as his daughter rooted against her mother's chest. His eyes flew to his wife's. She'd opened them. He couldn't see with the tears flowing down his cheeks. Katie moved slightly, her eyes fastening on their baby.

"Stop blubbering, Daniel Sullivan, and help me lift your wife up a little. She's been lying around long enough." Mrs. Grey supported Katie and the baby as Daniel helped lift her up slightly. Katie looked from her baby to Mrs. Grey. A gentle smile lit up the older woman's face. "You need to feed your little girl." The smile disappeared as Mrs. Grey turned her attention on the other occupants of the room. "Off you go now. Mrs. Sullivan needs to feed her daughter and she doesn't need the rest of you gaping at her. Out."

Nobody moved, causing Mrs. Grey to stand up and put her arms on her hips. "I said leave. My patient needs to be alone now. You all have jobs to do."

The others ran from the room leaving Daniel

staring at his neighbor. "Mrs. Grey, I don't, well the thing is..."

"You're welcome. Now leave. It's not seemly for you to be here. Your wife needs tending. You can come back later."

She ushered Daniel to the door, closing it behind him. He stood in the corridor staring at the door. If he hadn't witnessed it for himself, he would never have believed what just happened.

CHAPTER 38

*D*avy knew he should stay on the ranch rather than heading back to town. But he needed to be with Mary and the rest of his family. Why would God take Katie now? Her baby needed her. Daniel loved her. Mary would be devastated. Mary. He missed his wife. They had a fantastic time at the Harvest festival. She was the belle of the ball but hadn't looked at another man. Only him. He was lucky. He couldn't wait to make her truly his. But then what if she wanted a baby? He could be in Daniel's situation. *Stop it. Women have babies all the time. Yes, but some of them die.* Could he live with losing Mary? The loss of Tilly had nearly destroyed him and he hadn't been in love with her. *Love? Oh dear Lord, when had he fallen in love with Mary.*

As if he had conjured her up, he saw his wife running toward him from the store. He parked, his stomach churning as he searched her face. *Dear Lord, let Katie be ok.* Wiping his hands on his trousers, he held them out for his wife. "Katie?"

"She's alive. Doc says it's a miracle. Mrs. Grey did it. She saved Katie."

With a whoop of delight, Davy grabbed Mary and swung her around kissing her soundly.

"Davy, put me down." Mary said, giggling as her husband continued to turn her around.

HER GIGGLES STOPPED as he put her down but didn't release his hold. Instead, he pulled her closer. She turned her face up toward his, needing a kiss. She didn't care if he thought she was forward. After the stress of the last few days, she desperately needed to feel close to him. The kiss sent tingles down her body, melting her insides, as she pressed closer to him. Without releasing her, he moved her back against the wagon, his mouth ravaging hers. She moaned as her hands played in his hair. His whiskers scratched her skin but she didn't care. All she wanted was to show him how much she cared for him. She loved him and wasn't afraid anymore to show it. When he broke off their kiss, disappointment flooded over her.

"MARY, we should go. We are in the middle of the street." His heavy breathing made his voice all husky. She nodded, biting her lip as she gazed at him. With a low moan, he kissed her soundly before pulling away.

They walked arm in arm to the store where they found the new family waiting upstairs. Holding her niece, Mary looked up to find Davy looking at her, a look of longing in his eyes. She turned her focus back to the baby in front of her, giving her a cuddle before handing her back to her mother.

"Thank you." Katie said weakly. "Ma told me you looked after her and ran the boarding house so she could stay here."

"It was nothing. You did the hard work." Tears filled Mary's eyes as she took in the picture of her friend, brother-in-law and new baby, sitting together on the bed. *Thank you Lord.* She saw Katie, fighting to keep her eyes open. Looking up, she caught her husband's eye. "Ready to go home?" He mouthed. She nodded.

Mary snuggled into Davy's side as they rode home to the ranch. She dozed off more than once as the stress of the previous week took its toll. "Go to sleep, I won't let you fall off." Davy whispered as she jerked awake once more. The next morning she woke to find herself in her own room. She was only partially dressed. Her cheeks heated as she remembered Davy helping her to take off her dress before putting her to bed. She had wanted him to stay with her.

CHAPTER 39

Mary found Davy in the kitchen. Her smile fell as he didn't look up when she said good morning. *Maybe he didn't hear me.* "Are you planning on going into town today?"

"No, there is too much work to catch up on. One of the men is worried the cattle may be sick. I have to leave shortly."

"Oh." *Don't go, stay here with me.*

"I don't know how long I will be gone. Mrs. Higgins can take you into town if you want to go see Katie and the baby. "

"I'd rather wait till you get back." Mary said, trying to bridge the gap that seemed to have sprung up between them. Yesterday they had been so close, yet here they were almost strangers once more.

Davy didn't reply. He drained his coffee before

standing up and stalking out of the room. She stared after him through a mist of tears. What had happened?

DAVY RODE his horse but his mind was elsewhere. He couldn't look at Mary without wanting to take her to bed. He didn't think she was ready to be intimate just yet. He had to be patient but it was hard with her being so attractive. Last night, it had taken him every ounce of willpower not to stay with her. He knew she was tired out. The last few days had drained all of them. He didn't want to take advantage of her. *You could have been nicer this morning. You hurt her.* The wounded look in her eyes had stayed with him. *It wouldn't have hurt to have stayed with her today, would it? The ranch isn't going to run itself. That's why you have ranch hands.*

Davy cursed silently. Talking to himself was going to make him mad. He needed to cool down. He spurred the horse on toward the creek. A nice bath would help sort out his body.

MARY KEPT LOOKING out the window but there was no sign of Davy coming home. She had gone over and over the events of yesterday but it still didn't make sense. She was relieved when Mrs. H suggested a trip to town. She said she had to stock up on supplies, but both of them knew it was an excuse to meet the newest member of the Sullivan clan.

"You look well, Katie." Mary said, holding out her hands for the little bundle. "Has this little darling a name yet?"

Katie smiled at her daughter. "Ella Lorena Sullivan."

"Lorena. Isn't that Mrs. Grey's first name?" Mrs. H asked softly as she cooed at the baby.

"Yes, it is. It's only fitting especially after what she did."

Mary laughed. "I never thought I would see the day you named your child after that woman."

Katie's grin disappeared. "That woman has a name, Mary Ryan Sullivan. I owe her everything."

"Katie, I was only teasing. I know she was marvelous. I only wish I had seen Daniel's face when she came marching into the room. Ellen said he looked like he was fit to burst."

"I was, but I can't thank her enough now. When I think of what …" Daniel walked through the door, having heard the conversation. "Mrs. Grey saved my wife's life and will always be welcome in our home."

They all stared at the baby, thinking of what could have happened. The silence grew uncomfortable until Ella cried out.

"We don't want to think about bad things today." Katie took the baby back from Mary.

"Congratulations on your little girl, Daniel. She is going to be a looker."

"Thanks, Mrs. H, she takes after her Ma."

Katie exchanged a loving glance with Daniel. Mary pinned her smile in place although her heart hurt. Would Davy ever look at her like that? She doubted it. "We should go and let you rest. See you Sunday, Katie. Bye, Ella Lorena Sullivan. You be good for your ma." Mary kissed the baby on the cheek before walking out the door, closely followed by Mrs. H.

They rode home in comfortable silence for a while.

"Did you know Mrs. Grey was a nurse in the war?"

Mrs. H shook her head at Mary's question. "No, but thank goodness she was. I dread to think what would have happened if Ellen hadn't gone to get her. Wonder how she knew?"

"Seems Ellen took to visiting Mrs. Grey soon after Katie came here. Their Mam told the girls that people were only mean if life had given them a hard time. She said nasty people deserved help. Ellen took her advice to heart. At first, Mrs. Grey didn't want anything to do with her but....well, you know how persistent she can be."

"It must be an Irish trait. You all have it." Mrs. H joked. "Although Mrs. Grey has it too and she's from Scottish blood."

"Poor lady. She lived in Winchester with her family. Her son got caught in crossfire and died as a result of his wounds. She believes he could have lived if the hospital tents had nurses. She volunteered and nursed for the remainder of the war. Her low opinion of doctors was formed by what she saw."

"Poor Dr. Clayton. He does his best."

"I'm sure he does but don't say that to Mrs. Grey."

"Not likely. I like my head on my shoulders, thanks."

Mary smiled at the thought of Mrs. H taking on Mrs. Grey. It would be a formidable battle and she wasn't sure who would win.

CHAPTER 40

*T*he knock at the back door startled Mary. She rubbed her floury hands on her apron before walking out of the kitchen and down the hall to open it.

"Afternoon, Ma'am. Got that surprise you asked for."

"Oh, thank you, Mick. You are just in time. Davy has gone out for a while. Bring it in please."

Mick walked in carrying a shiny black leather saddle. It looked like new. Mary couldn't resist rubbing her fingers over the soft leather leaving a trail of flour. With a giggle, she wiped it off with the side of her apron before looking up at the ranch hand with glee. "Do you think he will like it?"

"Yes, Ma'am. I'm sure he'll love it. Special occasion,

is it?" Mick glanced in the direction of the cake she had baked now cooling on the table.

"It's his birthday tomorrow but I thought…" Mary blushed. "Mrs. Higgins is in town tonight so I baked him a cake."

"He's a lucky man, Mrs. Sullivan, if you don't mind me saying so. Not only got himself a pretty wife but also judging by the smell, a good cook too. Me and the boys wouldn't mind a piece of birthday cake. What time are you planning on cutting it?" Mick put the new saddle on a chair near the table.

Oh no, her plans didn't include inviting the ranch hands to dinner. She wanted it to be just the two of them. It was time they took their relationship to the next level. Mary stared at the floor, wondering how to tell the ranch hand it was a private affair. She looked up as Mick burst out laughing.

"Sorry but you should see the look on your face. Don't fret yourself Mrs. Sullivan, I was only teasing. The boys say I go too far."

"Not at all Mick and please stop calling me, Mrs. Sullivan. My name is Mary. Tell the boys I will have cake for them tomorrow. Don't let on to Davy about his birthday. He doesn't know I know."

Mick touched the side of his nose. "Secret is safe with me, Mrs.… I mean Mary. So where do you want the saddle? We don't want the boss to sit on it."

Mary thought for a second. "Would you mind taking it into the sitting room. I don't want to dirty it again. He doesn't usually go in there until later so it will stay a surprise."

Mick grinned picking up the saddle. "Just show me where you want it. So what part of Ireland are you from? My parents came over from Dublin."

Mary led the way from the kitchen down to the sitting room, chatting as she went. "I'm from Galway, same as Katie. Were you born here or in Dublin?"

"Here." Mick put the saddle on the sofa and the two of them walked toward the front door.

"Do your parents live nearby? You could invite them to the party on Saturday night. Ma, I mean Davy's Ma, loves talking to people from Ireland."

"They died some years back."

"Oh, I'm sorry." The door behind her opened.

* * *

"WHAT ARE YOU DOING HERE?" The door banged as Davy kicked it closed behind him.

"Oh Davy, I wasn't expecting you back this early." Mary looked flustered, her cheeks red. Guilty almost.

"Sorry, Boss. I came to ask you something but you weren't here. I got talking to Mary here about back

173

home. Seems she may…" Mick stopped talking in the face of Davy's stare.

Davy took a step forward, putting his arm around his wife's shoulders. The message was clear. *She's mine.* The silence grew uncomfortable. Mary twisted a cloth in her hands while Mick inched toward the door.

"Go on, you were saying. You were talking to Mary but I guess you mean Mrs. Sullivan, my wife." His menacing tone had the desired effect. Mick's adam's apple moved rapidly as he swallowed hard.

"I best get going." Mick said stuttering, tripping over his own feet in his haste to get out the door.

"Wait. What was so important that you had to come to see me at night?" Davy didn't bother to hide his anger.

"Oh, that. Um, well, I was going to ask a favor but it can wait."

"Spit it out, man. I am sure *Mary* is interested too."

"Davy, stop it, please. You are embarrassing all of us. Mr. Quinn was just leaving." Mary held the door open and almost pushed Mick out of it. She slammed it shut behind him and putting her hands on her waist turned on Davy. "What in heaven's name got into you? The man was just being friendly."

"Friendly, is that what you call it?"

"Aye, what else would you?"

He stormed out of the hall toward the kitchen, expecting her not to follow him.

"Davy Sullivan, don't you dare walk off on me. I demand to know what just happened. You were so rude to Mr. Quinn. He may just leave." They reached the kitchen. Mary picked up a plate, hoping he wouldn't spot the cake waiting to be decorated. She needn't have worried; he was too busy ranting to notice anything else.

"And what of it?"

"I don't understand. The other day you said there was nobody who knew cattle like Mick. Now you seem to want him to leave the ranch. It doesn't make sense."

"What do you care whether he goes or not? Unless he is not the stranger he appeared to be? Was he a beau from back east?" Davy regretted the words as soon as they were out of his mouth.

Mary dropped the plate she had just picked up, her face white with shock. "You think…. No, it's not … Oh my goodness." She stared at him for a few seconds; tears making her eyes look huge, before burying her face in her apron and rushing in the direction of the stairs.

CHAPTER 41

*H*e stalked after her but hearing the door slam, changed his mind. Maybe he should give her time to calm down. He turned back toward the kitchen. Where was Mrs. Higgins? She knew better than to let random strangers into the house. *Mick is hardly a stranger. He's been working here for about a year now.*

As Davy wandered back toward the kitchen, delicious smells he had been too worked up to notice previously, wafted toward him causing his stomach to rumble. Uh oh. Davy couldn't believe he had forgotten. Mary had suggested giving the housekeeper some time off and he'd agreed. She was in town visiting with friends. He'd wondered at Mary's enthusiasm to be rid of Mrs. Higgins but given the smell, she had been busy cooking dinner. Davy groaned. She obviously had planned an intimate dinner for the both of them. As if to prove his point, he only then noticed the table set for two. She had put out candles and flowers. Then he spotted the cake.

He could kick himself. No wonder she was so upset at his veiled accusations. Here, she'd been cooking and baking all afternoon by the look of it. Far too busy to be entertaining anyone, let alone another man. He had to trust her. She hadn't given him any reason to doubt her. But he had trusted Tilly and look where that got him. Mary wasn't Tilly. She was kind hearted and wanted to make a go of this marriage. *But you don't know that. She could be just stringing you along.* Davy put his head in his hands. *You are a fool, Davy Sullivan. Worse than that. A cad.* Causing a woman as fine as Mary to cry. Accusing her of all sorts of bad behavior. In front of the hired hand. No doubt his name would be mud in the bunkhouse tonight.

He had to make this right. He took the stairs two at a time.

CHAPTER 42

*H*e knocked on the bedroom door, cursing silently as he heard the muffled sounds of crying. "Mary, please let me come in."

"Go away."

His heart twisted as the sobbing got louder. "Mary, I'm sorry." He listened in silence wondering if she was going to reply.

"Go away. I never want to see you again."

Angry with himself, he twisted the doorknob desperate to prove to her he was sorry. The door wouldn't open, it looked as if she had pulled something up against it. "Mary, open the door. We have to sort this out. I'm your husband. You have to speak to me sometime."

"You're not my husband. You don't want me. You

never tried to… Well, you know. Go away. Please. Just go. "

Davy stood looking at the door. He could force it open but what would that achieve. He didn't want to scare her. But the thoughts of losing her didn't sit well either. She was his. He didn't want her to leave. He loved coming home in the evenings sharing time with her. He looked forward to their talks in front of the fire. He hadn't realized how lonely he was until Mary had come into his life. She was everything he ever wanted. Beautiful, smart, kind hearted and so attractive he had struggled to keep his hands off her. How could she believe he didn't want her? He had been afraid to show her in case he frightened her off. She had been so wary and shy with him. He wanted her to be comfortable before they shared a bed. He hit his forehead against the frame of the door. Had he waited too long? Did she really believe he didn't think of her as a wife?

"Mary, I'm sorry. I behaved like a… well, it's not fitting to put that into words. Please come out. Let's go downstairs and eat. The meal you made smells delicious." Nothing. But at least the sobbing seems to have stopped. "I'll do anything. Even eat my hat if you will just come out. Give me a chance, please. I know I don't deserve it. I will try to explain but I can't do that with a door between us." The door remained closed. "Mary

Sullivan, get yourself out here now. Do you not remember you promised to obey me? Well, I am telling you woman to get out here. Now!"

"Don't you dare start ordering me about you…you big lummox. You are in the wrong here. Not me."

Davy smiled. She was shouting at him – that was better than sobbing. "Mary, I said I'm sorry. Please come downstairs. We can have dinner and talk."

"Dinner. Oh no." She wailed. "It will be ruined. It's still in the oven."

"I will get it. Please come downstairs."

CHAPTER 43

*D*avy ran back downstairs into the kitchen and rescued the beef. It was only slightly overdone. He would tell her he preferred it that way. Anything to make her feel better, given the mess he had made of things so far. He heard footsteps coming down the hall but instead of waiting for her at the door, he got busy dishing up the meal.

"Is it ruined?" The sound of her voice hoarse from crying cut him to the bone.

"It turned out just the way I like it. Sit down, please, and let me serve you." She turned away from him but before she could protest, he said softly "Please." Mary sat but held her shoulders rigid. *Tread carefully, Davy. You only got one chance to put this right.* He set the plates in front of them and took his seat.

Silence reigned as they both played with their food, neither eating. "Thank you for all your effort. I am very sorry I ruined things."

"Why? What made you behave like that?"

The fire was back in her eyes. He clenched his hands before wiping them down his trousers. His mouth was so dry he could barely speak. Desperately he tried to find the words to explain things. "I need to tell you a story but it don't make for pleasant listening. Why don't we eat first and then take our coffee to the sitting room. I promise to try to make you understand."

She eyed him warily before saying. "You hurt me."

The simple statement made him feel worse than a heel. "I know. I would do anything to start today over again. I was a fool. Forgive me?"

"I'll try."

They picked up their forks again but after a few bites both pushed their plates away. "You go sit by the fire. I'll follow with the coffee."

SHE LOOKED at him as he took the plates to the sink. He was sorry. She knew that not just by his words but also from the emotions she saw warring in his eyes. It was hard to forgive him. She still couldn't believe he had treated her so badly but yet... he must have a reason. She had watched him with other people and the animals. He had a kind heart.

CHAPTER 44

She moved to the sitting room and sat watching the flames flickering. It brought back happy memories of sitting by the fireside with her parents. They had a good marriage, although it had not been a love match. Her grandparents had used the services of a local matchmaker. Was that much different to being a mail order bride? In theory, the matchmaker knew both families but in reality, the couple were strangers when they married. Just like herself and Davy. She listened for his footsteps. Maybe he is still trying to get his story straight.

She tried to put aside her hurt and anger. Her marriage had to work. She loved living in Clover Springs. For the most part, Davy was a good husband. He had provided her with a comfortable home, a housekeeper and hadn't made any demands on her person. So what if he had a tendency to lose his temper? That wasn't the worst fault in a man. She could learn to live with it? Couldn't she?

* * *

DAVY WALKED SLOWLY toward the sitting room. He had to make her understand. But how? By telling her the truth about Tilly. Nobody knew the secret. Well, only one person did and he wasn't about to spill the beans. If he shared Tilly's story, then he was disrespecting her memory. *If you don't, you will lose your wife.* He didn't want to lose Mary. He loved her. Davy stood still before entering the room. He didn't know when he had fallen in love with Mary but that didn't matter. He couldn't risk losing her. He would tell her everything and pray that she understood and could forgive him.

"I put cream and a little sugar in your coffee just the way you like it." He handed her the cup, noting with disappointment she didn't meet his eyes. 'Mary, I am sorry about today."

"So you've said. But it's not the first time you have acted strangely. It's like you don't… well, almost as if you think I shouldn't talk to another man."

"Why do you want to do that?"

"Do what?" She put her cup down, folding her arms across her chest.

Davy rubbed the back of his neck. He had done it again. Started another argument. This wasn't going well at all.

CHAPTER 45

"I have to tell you something I haven't told anyone. It's not really my story to tell but … well I hope you understand."

Mary nodded but remained silent.

"Did anyone tell you I was engaged before? Her name was Tilly. She came from over near Clear Creek. We met when Pa took me with him on a business trip. He was buying some horses for the ranch and he thought it would be good for me to learn the ropes." Davy knew he was waffling but it was hard.

"Anyway, we met and fell in love. Or at least I did. I thought she did too." He couldn't look at Mary; the hurt from reliving the story was too much. He stared into the fire. "Pa wasn't in favor of the match. He believed Tilly was too young and immature. Happen he was right but I was too headstrong to listen. I started courting her and made every excuse to make the trip over to see her." Davy fell silent, his mind remembering the raven-haired girl with the wide smile. She had been so full of fun.

"What did her Pa think?"

Mary's question focused Davy. "I think he agreed, although his priorities were elsewhere. He had a hankering to go prospecting for gold. Looking back, I think he was keen to get rid of Tilly. That would free him up to head to the mountains. He wasn't a bad man just not cut out to be a father. Tilly's Ma had died in childbirth so it was just the two of them."

"Wasn't there family that could take her if he wanted to leave so badly?"

Davy sensed Mary was trying her best to make it easier for him to tell the story but her questions were having the opposite effect. "No. It was just the two of them, as I said. Well, really, there were three."

"Three?"

"Tilly's uncle. He was from her Ma's younger brother. He was responsible for the Pa's interest in gold. He had found some nuggets in the claim he was working. Said he would share it with his family." Davy grimaced. He could feel the bile rising in his throat, as he got closer to the most painful part of the story.

Caught up in memories, he didn't sense Mary rise until he felt her by his side, her arm stroking his gently.

"You don't have to tell me. I can see it's painful."

"No, I have to. Maybe then you will understand. So Wilbur moved into the house with Tilly and her Pa. He seemed nice enough. Spent too much time in the local saloon for my tastes but it meant time alone with Tilly. I wasn't complaining. We were young and in love. Pa finally agreed to us setting a date. June 30th it would have been." Davy stopped, swallowing hard. He knew it would be difficult but this was worse than he expected.

"She died before your wedding. I'm sorry, Davy. I know she meant the world to you."

"No, Mary. I thought I was in love with her but now I know Pa was right. We were too young." He sat staring at his hands.

"Davy, you don't have to pretend. I didn't come here expecting a love match. I knew what I was letting myself in for when I agreed to become a mail order bride. Love stories are for fairy tales."

"Katie and Daniel found love. Couldn't we?"

Mary sat straighter moving slightly away from him. He turned toward her, taking her hand in his. Not wanting to scare her.

"Mary, I love you."

"What? You can't. I mean, the way you behaved earlier. That's not love." Mary stood up. "I think it's time I retired."

Davy shot to his feet. "Please don't go yet. I need to tell you the ..."

Frantic knocking on the front door interrupted them. "What on earth..." Davy got to the door just as Mick walked in shouting for him.

"Boss, you got to come now."

"Can't it wait." Davy stared at his ranch hand.

"Sorry, boss. Luke is dead, I've sent Jeb for the sheriff."

"Dead? How?"

"Rustlers. He didn't have a chance to draw his gun."

Mary cried out. "Luke, the poor man. Oh no, Sorcha. He was writing to her. I think he asked her to marry him in his last letter."

Davy had to go, although his instinct was to stay with Mary and protect her. "Mary, I've got to ride with the men. I heard Mrs. H come back from town earlier. I'll send her to you. Don't leave the house. For any reason. Not until I get back."

"But..."

"Mary, don't argue with me. Not now. It's dangerous out there."

Mary nodded. Davy gave her a quick kiss on the

cheek before following Mick outside. Mary ran after them.

"Davy, please be careful."

Davy nodded before jumping on the horse Mick had brought for him.

CHAPTER 46

avy urged the horse to go faster, hoping Jeb had found the sheriff. He couldn't believe they had come back again. He'd thought they'd be wary of being caught, given one of their gang was in prison waiting for the judge. They didn't know how many men were in the gang. Mick said Luke was dead when Henry got to them. His mouth tightened. He spurred his horse on eager to catch up with his men. Luke had been a good man, one of the best ranch hands he had. Anger made him reckless so he forced himself to think rationally. Luke would be avenged. The cattle he had lost could be replaced. He hoped his scout was right in thinking the rustlers had left. He didn't want to consider what would happen should they double back and find Mary alone. *She isn't alone.*

Mrs. H is with her and a couple of the boys. Jeb would bring more people out from the town. Daniel may even take Mary to stay with Katie until this trouble blew over.

* * *

MARY AND MRS. H sat up late drinking coffee. They had cried over Luke. Mrs. H had written to his parents. It was up to Mary to write to Sorcha. She didn't know what to say, so decided to wait until she could speak to Katie.

"Did you know Tilly?" Mary asked Mrs. H watching her reaction very closely. Mrs. H busied herself with the cups. She didn't answer. "Mrs. H. Davy told me a little about her but then we got interrupted."

"Her death nearly tore that boy apart. He seemed to blame himself but there was nothing he could do. The good Lord called her back." Mrs. H stayed silent for a couple of seconds, as if wondering what she should say next.

"Mary, don't you be comparing yourself to young Tilly. You are a woman. She was just a girl. She is his past. You are his future."

"Am I?"

When Mrs. H didn't look up at her, Mary colored. "Sorry Mrs. H, I shouldn't have said that."

"Miss Mary, it isn't any of my business really, but I want Davy to be happy. You make him smile. I like looking at him watching you."

"He doesn't, well, it's just that he seems to... Oh never mind. I shouldn't say it."

"He gets jealous of you talking to the men. He shouldn't, as you've never looked twice at one of them. You love him, don't you?"

Mary was too embarrassed to look up.

"You stay true to your feelings, Miss Mary, but don't let Davy get away with treating you badly. You have to stand up to him and show him how you feel."

"How do I do that?" Mary looked at her shaking hands. She clasped them together, wishing she had a cold towel for her face. "I've never been with a man. Not properly. I don't know how to show him I love him."

"That's easy, darling. You bought him the saddle. Wasn't he pleased?"

"I am not sure he saw it. He, well... he didn't like the fact Mick was here when he came home."

Mrs. H pursed her lips. "There's times when I want to put Davy over my knee and spank him."

Mary giggled at the fierce expression on Mrs. H's

face. Mrs. H started laughing too before standing up. "It's time for bed but tomorrow I will teach you how to make apple pie just as Davy likes it. My mama always said the way to a man's heart was through his stomach."

CHAPTER 47

The apple pie turned out perfectly. Mary tried to be happy but she was worried about her husband. She loved him. Yes, he had issues with jealousy. If she wanted to stay with him, she would have to learn to live with it. *He should trust me.* With effort, Mary dampened down her angry thoughts. No marriage was perfect. The best were based on compromise. *And trust.* Where was the trust between her and Davy? *He doesn't believe you are faithful. How can a relationship work without faith?* Mary paced backwards and forwards. Mrs. H gave her jobs to do but the time dragged by. *Where was Davy? Was he safe?*

They heard horses outside and ran out to check. Mary tried to curb her disappointment. She was pleased to see Jeb was unhurt. He had brought Daniel and some other men from town. The men would ride after Davy. Daniel tried to persuade Mary to return to town with him but she refused.

"My place is by Davy's side, Daniel."

"He'd prefer you in town, Mary."

"This is my home and I'm not leaving."

Daniel wasn't happy but he had to get back to Katie and the store. After he left, Mary watched as Mrs. H cleaned an old rifle. "Do you think there will be trouble?"

"Not really, Miss Mary, but it's best to be prepared."

Mary wished she had paid more attention to the lessons Davy had given her, but even now, she wasn't sure she would be able to shoot someone. "Have you ever shot someone, Mrs. H?"

Mrs. Higgins nodded. "Long time back. Before we came to live here."

"Did they die?" Mary shuddered but she wanted to know.

"I wouldn't be here if they didn't. They killed my husband and I wasn't about to let them get me or the boys. God knows where my boys would have ended up. I didn't want them living with the Apache."

"Indians? But I thought they were friendly."

"They are around here but it was different back

before the war. I don't really blame the Indians; they were just protecting what they thought was theirs. White men took their land and they wanted it back."

The days passed by slowly. She helped with different chores. Mrs. H was a good teacher, always patient, which was good as Mary couldn't concentrate on anything. Mrs. H told her stories of growing up in the South before the war years. Her family had lived on the edge of a large plantation.

"You should have seen the parties, Miss Mary. People came from miles around. The ladies wore huge gowns and their jewelry sparkled like snow on the mountain top." Mary sat mesmerized as the housekeeper painted a picture of years gone by. "I was friendly with one of the little girls at the plantation. Her Mama and Daddy were away a lot and she was lonely. I shouldn't have been anywhere near that house. I used to climb in her bedroom window."

Mary giggled.

"I know it's hard to believe I was capable of that but I wasn't always old you know. Anyway, this night there was a big dance. We hid behind some curtains in the room where the ladies got dressed. You should have seen those girls. They were so pretty. Their maids tied their stays so tight, I didn't know how they could breathe, never mind dance, but they did."

"Did your father own slaves?"

"No, Miss Mary, we didn't have the money to own slaves. He agreed with it though. It was another thing we fought about."

"My Daddy and I never fought. I didn't think he was able to fight but then he got mixed up with the freedom fighters. He died because of them." Mary took a deep breath, trying not to let the tears start as she didn't know if she could stop them. She needed to distract herself. "How did you meet your husband? Was he at one of those balls?"

Mrs. H laughed, her belly moving up and down as she struggled to regain her composure. "My Tom never saw inside a plantation. He was from the North. Yet another thing I did to upset Daddy. I met Tom when he came to visit his cousins. We ran away together."

"You must have loved him very much."

"Yes, I did. It was hard with him being a northerner and me from the south. Especially during the war. That's when we decided to move West. We had the boys to consider. We wanted a better life for them. But it wasn't to be." Mrs. H fell silent, her eyes closed. Mary didn't say anything. She waited until the older woman was up to talking again. "Daddy never forgave me so I couldn't go back home after Tom died in the

Indian raid. That's how I ended up on the Sullivan ranch with two young boys and not a penny to my name. If it wasn't for Mr. Sullivan, Davy's father, I don't know what would have happened to me and my kids."

CHAPTER 48

"*W*as it worth it?" Mary asked, before putting her hand over her mouth. "I'm sorry. Don't answer."

"Yes, it was. We had a good marriage. Of course, we fought but then we got to kiss and make up."

Mary's cheeks flushed at the dreamy expression on the other woman's face.

"It wasn't all sunshine and roses. There were times when I would have gone home if I could. But marriage is like that, honey. It takes two people to work at it. Men are different to us women. They don't always use their brains the way they should. They seem to think we will know what's going on in their heads just by looking at them."

Mary wanted to ask Mrs. H more, but she couldn't. She didn't want to embarrass the other woman. It would be difficult to admit Davy wasn't really her husband. Not in the true sense of the word. She bit her lip. It wasn't right to discuss her marriage with anyone.

"Davy took after him. He has the same kind heart and will treat you just as well as his Pa treated his Ma."

Mary's skepticism must have shown on her face as Mrs. H rubbed her arm. "Give him a chance to explain child. Let him say he's sorry and forgive him. You love him. Anyone can see that. He is a man worth fighting for."

Mary went to bed, considering the housekeepers advice. She had spent the nights praying for her husband to return. She prayed even harder. "I'll be patient and never say a harsh word again, Dear Lord. Just bring him home safe."

The sound of horses interrupted their dinner the next day. They both rushed to the door to find the men outside. Davy jumped down but didn't move toward Mary. He started to but then stopped.

"Did you get them?" Mrs. H asked.

"We did."

"So, what's with the long face?"

"They weren't cattle rustlers. Well, they were but not the hardened type. It was a father and his sons. The boys were barely teenagers. They said their family was starving and they had to steal cattle to eat. At

least, that's what I think they said. They didn't speak a
lot of English."

"Why did they kill Luke?"

"One of the boys did it. Seems he got scared and his
gun went off. It was an accident really. Not that it's
going to help Luke or his family."

"What will happen to them?" Mary asked, not
really wanting to know the answer.

"They'll hang. Stealing cattle is a crime. It doesn't
matter what their reasons were."

Mary said a quick prayer for the families of the
rustlers and Luke. She had liked the quiet ranch hand.
Davy looked tired and sad. *He really does have a kind
heart.* "I made you an apple pie. Why don't you wash
up and I will put dinner on the table?" Mary looked at
the ranch hands. "You are all welcome to join us."

CHAPTER 49

*D*avy hung back as the ranch hands rushed to wash up. They were starving and the prospect of good hot food was tempting. Davy wasn't hungry. He hadn't eaten anything but jerky since leaving Mary. His stomach was doing somersaults while he stared at his wife. Mary worked hard and had turned his house into a home. Everyone loved her. Mrs. Higgins sang her praises all the time.

He couldn't tell from looking at her face whether she was still angry with him. He had treated her so badly the night of his birthday. On the trail, he had gone over and over his behavior, wondering how to fix the damage his jealousy had caused. He had no right to question his wife's virtues. She had never given him any reason not to trust her. He had told her he loved her. She hadn't said how she felt. Mick had interrupted them before she could. He rubbed his sweaty hands down his trousers. He had to talk to her again. But now wasn't the time. They needed privacy. He couldn't risk being interrupted a second time. Sighing loudly, he led his horse to the barn.

Sometime later, the barn door opened and Mrs. H walked in. "So this is where you are hiding."

"I'm not hiding. I had to look after the horses. We rode them hard."

"Humph. You're the boss. You could have got the men to do that. I know you, Davy Sullivan. You're scared."

Davy didn't answer. He pushed his head closer to the horse he was rubbing down. The last thing he needed was a lecture from Mrs. H.

"You have a good woman in there. Someone who was scared stiff the whole time you were away. You should be in the house giving her a great big hug, not hiding out here."

"She probably doesn't want me anywhere near her. I didn't exactly behave the night of the raid."

"You sure didn't. You let that green-eyed monster come out again. You got to get a control of that, Davy, before you lose the best thing that ever happened to you. Mary loves you."

"She does?" Davy's heart swelled with hope.

"Yes, she does, you half-wit. Now, what are you going to do about it?"

"I need to speak to her. In private."

"I'm not going to send her out here. You stink. Get a bath and I will make more coffee. Don't be long."

"Yes, Ma'am." Davy grabbed Mrs. H and gave her a hug, before running off.

CHAPTER 50

*M*ary entered the living room but on seeing Davy, she turned to leave. Davy shot to his feet. "Please don't go yet. I want to apologize. I behaved very badly the night of my birthday." He looked at her but she stared into the fire.

"Thank you for my present. It's beautiful. Mick told me there was nothing between you. How Mrs. H organized the whole thing."

"So you take his word over mine. Thank you so much." Mary's anger was obvious, not only from her tone, but by the look on her face.

"No, that's not what I meant." Davy panicked. "I have to tell you the rest. Please sit."

She sat at the edge of the seat, her discomfort obvious.

"I love you, Mary. I know that's hard to believe but I do."

"Sure you do. That's why you didn't come in for dinner after being away for the last few days. I was worried about you. I thought you might die."

Davy smiled. "You were worried. I'm glad."

Mary's eyebrow lifted.

"I don't mean I'm glad you were upset. But just that you missed me. Oh, I am making a mess of this again. I am not good with words."

"How did Tilly die?"

"She fell down the stairs."

"Oh, the poor girl. How tragic. You must have been heartbroken." Mary's eyes filled with tears. Davy wiped a couple that spilled down her cheek. She reached up to stop him and he took her hand gently in his, using his other hand to cup her face. "Don't cry please, Mary. Not yet. The worst is to come."

"What could be worse?"

"Tilly's death wasn't an accident." He heard Mary's intake of breath. "At least, I don't believe it was. She killed herself and it's all my fault."

"Why? Suicide is a sin. It's not right or fair to say somebody did that unless you have proof. Do you?"

"Not exactly, but she had reason. She was pregnant."

Mary shuddered and sat back, putting as much

distance between them as possible. "With your baby? Why didn't you marry her? Oh the poor girl. May God have mercy on her soul."

"It wasn't mine."

"What? But… Well, I thought she was your fiancée? Oh..."

"Tilly was in love with someone else. Somebody she could never have. She had to marry someone and she chose me."

"Why you? One thing I have learned is that there are plenty of single men around."

"I lived in another town. I was her ticket to respectability. Although she was only 18, it turned out my so-called immature fiancée wasn't as innocent as Pa believed. "

"Couldn't the father of the child marry her?"

"He wasn't interested. His parents were the richest people in town and he was headed East to college. Poor Tilly believed his lies."

CHAPTER 51

*M*ary stared into the flames, her heart breaking for the poor girl. She could so easily have been in her position. She shivered, thanking the Good Lord she had the strength to deny the masters son's demands back in Ireland. She didn't know what to say to Davy. Part of her wanted to give him a hug and tell him it wasn't his fault but the other part wanted to know why he hadn't married the girl anyway. If he loved her, surely he should have helped her out of the situation.

"You are wondering why I didn't marry her anyway, aren't you?"

Surprised he read her mind, she could only nod.

"I had decided to do just that. I was on my way over to her place when I met her uncle in town. He was coming out of the saloon. He shot at me but thankfully he'd had so much liquor, he missed. Turns out he suspected Tilly was pregnant and had confronted her. She told him I took advantage of his absence but wasn't prepared to marry her. He held me responsible for her death. I think he knew she did it on purpose, too. "

"Oh, Davy. I'm sorry."

"I should never have told her I was breaking our engagement. If I had married her like she begged me to, she wouldn't be dead." He put his head in his hands, but not before she saw the tears glistening.

Mary put her arms around him as his shoulders heaved. "Don't, my darling. You are not responsible for Tilly. She made her own choice." She stroked his head, her own tears falling. "You weren't to know what she would do. You changing your mind shows you to be the kindhearted man I love."

He stilled and looked up at her.

"You do?"

Mary leaned down and kissed him gently on the lips. "Yes I do."

He put his arms around her, dragging her down on top of him. They toppled off the sofa and onto the rug in front of the fire. Her skin tingled as he brushed the loose tendrils of hair away from her face. His eyes held hers as he leaned toward her, stealing a kiss.

"I…love… you." Each word was punctuated with a kiss.

The kisses gradually changed from gentle to demanding as their breathing deepened. She gasped as he kissed his way from her lips to her ear and back. "You smell so good."

"Hmmm" She moaned, her ability to talk compromised by his demanding mouth.

All too soon, he seemed to realize he was lying on top of her. Without losing his hold, he picked her up and sat on the sofa with her on his knee.

"About earlier."

"Let's not talk about that." She looked at his lips willing him to kiss her again.

"Can you see now why I get jealous if you are with another man?"

Mary traced his face with her finger. "I do and I understand given what you have shared." As the relief flared in his eyes, she continued. "But you have to let the past go Davy. I am not Tilly. I am in love with you. Nobody else."

"I will try."

"You have to do better than that. I admit when we married, we were strangers. I thought you were handsome."

He silenced her with a kiss. Flustered, she had to think about what she'd been saying.

"And kind, if rather smelly." They both smiled.

'Since then, you have conquered my heart. I love you and only you. I want to be your wife." Embarrassed she looked down but cupping his hands on her face, he forced her to look at him.

"What are you saying, Mary?"

"You know."

"Maybe but I need to be sure." He kissed her. "Are you trying to say you are ready to be my wife in every sense?"

She nodded, her mouth too dry to speak even if she could concentrate on anything other than wanting to be kissed again. Her insides felt as if they had melted.

Grinning, he picked her up and walked toward the stairs.

EPILOGUE

*M*ary held her hands out in front of her. "Davy, I can't see a thing. I'll fall."

"You won't. Just hold tight. You'll ruin the surprise if you take off the blindfold."

"I must look a fright. You're a big child, Davy Sullivan." She poked her husband in the ribs. "Why did you come to town? Katie and I can meet Sorcha off the train. Haven't you got chores to do?"

Davy laughed louder but still refused to remove the cloth around his wife's eyes. The train would be here any minute. He couldn't wait to see her reaction. He spotted his sister-in-law and niece up ahead. Guiding Mary gently, he walked up to the rest of his family. Katie winked at him before teasing Mary.

"Morning. Not sure that fashion is going to catch on, Mary."

"Are you in on this too, Katie Sullivan? What is on the train? Is Cathy coming? No, she can't be as she is visiting Europe. Can you believe my little sister will see Paris?"

"Clover Springs is much nicer than Paris. What does Sorcha look like?"

Davy appreciated Katie's effort to change the subject. Mary still found it difficult to accept Cathy had a new family now.

"Sorcha. She's got blonde curly hair and is about this tall." Mary gestured with her hands. "Oh, I hate surprises."

"You love them and you know it. Shush up now or you'll wake Ella. If you do, you can get her back asleep."

Davy looked at the sleeping baby. Angelic was only used when she was asleep. Awake the child was as cranky as her namesake. At nine months old, it was easy to see who was the boss at the mercantile.

"It's coming. I can hear the whistle. What did you get me Davy? Is it a new book?" Mary jumped up and down in excitement.

"Patience is a virtue, wife. Didn't the good nuns teach you that?" He moved his foot out of his wife's way just in time.

"Oh look, there's Mr. Petersen now. Doesn't he

look smart?" Katie pointed out their neighbor who stood further along, playing with his hat.

"Looks rather nervous, if you ask me. It's not the wind shaking that hat. Reverend Tim may have to bolt the doors of the church for that service. Poor man, he should run now while he has the chance. While he's still free. Ow!" Davy rubbed his shin ruefully.

"You deserved it. What a way to talk. Anyone would think you hated being married. Mr. Petersen was delighted when Katie offered to write to Mrs. Gantley on his behalf. Wasn't he, Katie?"

"I'm not sure he was over the moon but he knows he needs a wife. It was fortunate Sorcha decided she wanted to come to Clover Springs as Mrs. Gantley didn't have anyone suitable. His children need a mother and he has to work or he will lose customers. People only have so much patience." Katie moved Ella onto her other shoulder.

"And some have none, isn't that right, Mary?" Davy couldn't resist teasing his wife but he wisely kept his feet out of her range this time. "Here's the train, on time for once."

The screech of the train brakes drowned out his words. Doors opened allowing the passengers to disembark. He spotted the boy immediately, his face alight with a mixture of excitement and terror. His companion was a nice looking girl with strawberry blonde hair. She, too, looked terrified although she was trying to smile.

"Wait here with Katie. I'll just be a minute." He took off before Mary could protest. Striding up to the girl holding the little boy's arm, he held out his hand. "Miss Matthews?"

The girl nodded, although her eyes filled with confusion. Swallowing hard, she whispered "Mr. Petersen?"

"No sorry, Miss. I'm Davy Sullivan, Mary's husband. This must be Ben. Thank you for looking after him on the journey." Davy looked around him for a minute. He couldn't see Petersen in the crowds. "Why don't you both come with me? Mary can't wait to see you. She's over there with Katie, my sister in law. Petersen will find us, he may have gone to get your bags."

"I have everything I own right here, Mr. Sullivan. Perhaps he was delayed." The girl looked around her, the mask hiding her fear slipping somewhat. Davy wanted to reassure her by telling her Brian Petersen was a nice man. But he couldn't. He didn't know him that well. The Petersen's hadn't lived in Clover Springs that long before the tragedy happened. "No, he's here all right. I saw him not five minutes ago. Please come with us. Katie can't wait to hear how Nellie is."

The smile on Sorcha's face widened. "Nellie told Cook to tell me to watch out for Indians."

Davy laughed loudly, causing a few people to stare in their direction. Davy bent down to be closer to the boy. "You must be Ben. I'm very pleased to meet you. Mary has told me lots about you." The boy stood taller. "She doesn't know you are coming, Ben. She thinks I've bought her some new books. I didn't tell her the Nuns let you come to live with us. She is going to be so happy. She told me all about you."

The child's face lit up with the biggest smile. Davy had to swallow hard to get rid of the lump in his throat. He held out his hand. "Come on, son. Let's go over to meet your new Ma."

Davy walked slowly towards Mary, trying to adjust his pace to match Ben's limp without making it too obvious. Sorcha walked slightly ahead of them. Katie's eyes widened when she saw the young boy. Davy put a finger to his lips to warn Katie to be quiet. He didn't want the surprise ruined now.

"Miss Matthews, would you mind taking off Mary's blindfold please." Davy and Ben exchanged grins.

"Sorcha, I am so glad you are here. Sorry about my husband. He has an odd sense of humor. I don't know what you thought you were doing Davy..." Mary turned toward her husband but stopped talking to stare at Davy and Ben.

"Oh my. Ben, what are you doing here?"

Davy watched as his wife bent down to give the child a big hug. Tears ran down her face.

"Go on son, give your new Ma a hug."

"Ma? You mean... Ben is ..."

Davy put his arm around Mary, kissing her on the cheek. "That's right. Ben is coming to live with us. Now stop fussing woman and take your son to the church. We need to find Petersen for Miss Matthews. We have a wedding to get to." Davy was nearly knocked off his feet as his wife gave him a huge hug.

"I love you Davy Sullivan."

THANK you so much for reading Mary. I hope you want to continue reading about those who live in Clover Springs. Sorcha the next book brings back old friends and introduces new ones.

Orphan Train Escape

Orphan Train Trials

Orphan Train Christmas

Orphan Train Tragedy

Orphan Train Strike

Orphan Train Disaster

Trail of Hearts - Oregon Trail Series

Oregon Bound (book 1)

Oregon Dreams (book 2)

Oregon Destiny (book 3)

Oregon Discovery (book 4)

Oregon Disaster (book 5)

12 Days of Christmas - co -authored series.

The Maid - book 8

Clover Springs Mail Order Brides

Katie (Book 1)

Mary (Book 2)

Sorcha (Book 3)

Emer (Book 4)

Laura (Book 5)

Ellen (Book 6)

ACKNOWLEDGMENTS

This book wouldn't have been possible without the help of so many people. Thanks to Erin Dameron-Hill for my fantastic covers. Erin is a gifted artist who makes my characters come to life.

Special thanks go to Nancy Cowan, Marlene Larsen, Cindy Nipper, Marilyn Cortellini, Sherry Masters, Janet Lessley, Robin Malek, Meisje Sanders Arcuri and Denise Cervantes who all spotted errors (mine) that had slipped through.

Come join us at https://www.facebook.com/groups/rachelwessonsreaders

Last, but by no means least, huge thanks and love to my husband and my three children.

Made in the USA
Middletown, DE
21 September 2024

61203025R00138